Meskwaki Burial Mounds

And Other Stories From Quinlan, Iowa,

The Eternal Town Where The Corn

Goddess Rules

By

G. Louis Heath, Ph.D.

G. Louis Heath

BK
$11.00

1stBooks – rev. 01/09/01

For my students at Mount St. Clare
College, Clinton, Iowa

"Mounties" we all

ABOUT THE BOOK

Twenty-two of the 24 stories in the book are about fictional Quinlan, Iowa near where a cult worships the Corn Goddess deep in the tall corn. In Quinlan, the golf course that covers Meskwaki burial mounds figures into the grotesque death of little, ten-year-old Jimmy Zelinski. Here also, middle-aged women become hopelessly addicted to the casino on the riverboat, The Mud Cat. It is a nether, other, perhaps higher world where cats fly and die, put into orbit in the most medieval fashion. It is the town where Olav, the Norwegian, kills in order to assert his Norwegian-ness. And Quinlan is near that special place in the corn where Hog Scent #30 has a special meaning that Chanel would have never dared dream.

Quinlan is also home to the Apostolic Church of Eternal Heaven that proselytizes the entire community with Jesus-rock music blaring from roof speakers 24 hours a day until an unlikely peacemaker emerges from the pages of the local phone directory. It is also where a romantic date turns bloody in the story "Deer Blood." And it is where young Jess Brownmiller bridges the generation gap with 81-year-old Thelma Carson after she runs a stop sign and collides with his car.

Quinlan is the home of Odin College, a Norwegian Lutheran institution, where Professor Rupert P. Hayes assigns his Sociology 322-X, "Garbology In The Modern World" class, to search residents' garbage at 3 a.m., only to get them involved in a murder. Readers will also experience the deeply moving story of Virginia Finseth, the only female wrestler at Odin College. You will also meet Odin's computer technician, Andrew, who attempts to "fix the minds" of students Dustin and Phil. And you will learn how blood got on the 30-foot-tall cemetery obelisk across the street from the college.

This is Quinlan, Iowa and Odin College in all their dark and light facets. The stories here report to you the best and most interesting of the town and its college and people.

Two non-Quinlan stories, "The Lynching Of The Mysterious Wyoming Cowboy" and "Our Soldier," are offered for your reading pleasure. Also, one story is included about Odin College's local competitor, Quinlan Community College, wherein Professor David Ward devises an ingenious plot to kidnap the college president. (The punch bowl at the 7th annual QCC spring semester party plays a pivotal role in this story.)

G. L. H.

Table of Contents

Olav, Norwegian

Quinlan, Iowa Police Chief Delbert Venzke held the mysterious note over the body and examined it. It read: **"NO REG, SO TAB RODER."** Inked in tiny block letters on a small square of white paper, it had been found beside the body.

Chief Venzke took a draw on his cigarette, puckered his brow, and racked his brain, trying to make sense of the letters. It didn't make any sense. He turned to his colleague, officer Bill Williams, who extended an open clear plastic bag toward the Chief. Venzke carefully deposited the note into the bag with the tweezers with which he held the note.

"Better get the forensics guys over here," ordered the Chief. "This looks like a difficult one. Try to get some prints off the note. Then fine-comb the body and the scene."

Williams, in his twenties, half the Chief's age, gave his assent with his usual "Yeah," a conversational signature so laconic and off-putting that it had initially irritated the Chief when Williams joined the Quinlan, Iowa Police Department two years ago. But now that he knew Williams, and had become friends with him, his less than appealing, emotionally bland style could be put in context. He theorized that Williams, basically a nice guy, liked to distance himself from the horrors and traumas of police work. With a body lying before them, who could blame them?

"NO REG?" The Chief scratched his head. "No regulation? That sounds reasonable," he noted. "But what about the **SO TAB RODER?** That doesn't look like anything remotely familiar."

Williams had just completed calling forensics on his cell phone. As he sheathed the phone, he suggested, "But maybe it isn't English. Maybe it's one of those Slavic languages. After all, hundreds of Bosnians, Serbs, Croats, and Kosovars have come to this state in the past few years."

1

The Chief seemed a bit nonplussed. "Hmmm. Maybe this is one of those Balkan ethnic rivalries imported to the heartland. That would be something, to have a bit of the Yugoslav mayhem dumped into our cornfield." The Chief put his cigarette aside and pulled on a pair of latex gloves. "It's about time we checked the identity of this guy. Is he really who they say he is?" He reached down and finagled the wallet out of the back pocket and opened it, thumbing through several cards in clear plastic foldout pockets, until he found the driver's license. He studied it a moment, then asked dryly, "Yes, it is who they claim. I recall the name now. Does Leonard Swanson sound Serbian to you?"

Williams shook his head. "It sounds American Iowan to me. Shoot that theory down."

Very elderly, Swanson had been found by his daughter on the floor of his room in the Vasa Nursing Home, a facility operated by the Sons of Sweden exclusively for its members. It had been named after the famous warship Vasa that had sunk over three hundred seventy years ago in Stockholm Harbor, and which had been raised, preserved, and displayed in a harborside museum in recent years. The Sons of Sweden had always served as a kind of mutual aid society for Swedish-Americans, offering insurance policies and small business loans, among other services. Now, as its membership had aged, it had for some time been building and administering nursing homes. Some voices in the community had been raised against this ethnic segregation. Yet, nothing had come of it since the Vasa Nursing Home was private, though a few of its residents, who had exhausted their resources, were covered by Title 19 federal assistance.

If Swanson had been found anywhere else, the location might have suggested a lead. This scene suggested nothing. If forensics established a suspicious cause of death, perhaps things would begin to add up. But as it stood, Swanson could have written the mysterious inked letters as part of a self-styled scrabble game some time before he fell dead of a stroke. If anyone had murdered him, he had not disturbed the room.

2

The Chief scratched his chin. He had a vague feeling that looking into Swanson's death could possibly become very interesting.

The lab report came back a little less than twenty-four hours later. Swanson's body had Agent Orange in it. His stomach also contained some kind of bread and some sort of berries eaten shortly before his death.

Chief Venzke tapped the lab report lying on his office desk with a pencil as he swigged some coffee from the huge mug he had bought at an Iowa Barnstormers indoor "arena football" game. He thought that this death might have something to do with Vietnam as the herbicide Agent Orange was widely used in the war to defoliate areas thought to harbor Vietcong. But Swanson was 89 years old, a veteran of World War II, and he had no son who had served in Vietnam. Perhaps he had simply decided to end it all by ingesting Agent Orange, easily purchased under the commercial brand name, "Roundup," in hardware stores. And before that, he had eaten a little bread and some berries. To absorb the Agent Orange? That did not make sense, nor did it help to explain the **"NO REG"** note, which suspiciously bore fingerprints that were not Swanson's. So, just possibly, this was a homicide that the perpetrator hoped looked like a suicide.

Of course, the fingerprints might be Swanson's daughter's, or those of a friend who had penned a message to the near-blind, very hard-of-hearing octogenarian. The daughter or a friend might have a motive. Venzke brushed the backside of his forefingers across his chin. Yes, just maybe, he might be able to construe the death as a homicide. In any event, he would have to look carefully at all possible angles. He had to assume murder until his investigation proved otherwise.

Venzke put on his raincoat and hat and left his office for his ten a.m. interview with Bodil Swanson, the daughter. What an odd name, "Bodil," thought Venzke as he exited the police station. And just how in the hell was he to pronounce it?

The Chief had learned from the editor of the local newspaper, the **Quinlan Quotient**, that Bodil had never married and that she was something of a Swedophile. That is a person who adores Sweden, her culture, people, just everything about the country. He had looked it up in the dictionary, where he had found the combination form "-phile," which means someone who almost obsessively likes the thing just preceding "-phile."

You learn something new everyday in this job, thought Venzke, including the fact that ethnicity was not just something for the recently arrived Vietnamese and Bosnians. The **Quinlan Quotient** had told him that this Swanson woman had gotten the very Swedish woman's name, "Bodil," from her Swedish immigrant father Lennart Swanson, who had grudgingly changed Lennart into the American Leonard in order to enhance his prospects for upward mobility. But the name Bodil, pronounced "Boo-dill," did not lend itself much to Americanization unless you wanted to invite unkind contrasts to the once eminent sex-symbol movie icon, Bo Derek, whose "Bo" was pronounced a little differently anyway.

Leonard Swanson had been born in south central Sweden, on a farm near the town of Gavle in the province of Dalarna. He had immigrated to the United States in 1908 in order to escape the grinding poverty then besetting Sweden, long before it had any serious thoughts of becoming an affluent welfare state. Like many immigrants of the era, he had never wanted to leave his homeland. (He had wept as his best friend saw him off at dockside as he embarked the Cunard Line's **Thor**, having paid 66 dollars for steerage across the Atlantic and a train ride to Uncle Sven's farm in eastern Iowa, total, both forms of transportation included for one price.)

Once in Iowa, he had intended to build a healthy bank account and return to Sweden well-off. But he soon married and Bodil arrived not long thereafter, fixing him in place with responsibilities. Yet, he still intended to return to Sweden someday with his family, and Bodil was named to reinforce her

4

Swedish ethnicity and facilitate her eventual participation in Swedish society. That, of course, had not happened. The local ruffians at Quinlan High had mispronounced her name and taken malicious delight in calling her "the boc," mocking her, making her school career an ordeal.

Bodil Swanson, clad in a bright blue-and-yellow (the national colors of Sweden) housedress, answered the doorbell. Chief Venzke took his hat off, announced who he was, and was admitted to a pleasant though unusual living room featuring all-yellow walls and all-light-blue chairs and sofa. Bodil extended her arm toward one of the blue Swedish modern chairs, and invited, "Please have a seat."

After he sat down, she offered him coffee. "Good Swedish coffee," she observed. "I get it from an import shop here in Quinlan."

Venzke stirred in sugar. He noted it came in a packet printed with words that could be none other than Swedish. "Socker" had to be Swedish for sugar.

Bodil Swanson said she wanted to solve her father's murder as soon as possible. (Or, perhaps she wanted to seem enthusiastic in so claiming in order to exclude herself as a suspect.) She told the Chief she did not pen the cryptic note. Venzke was inclined to believe her, given the finger print evidence, but he was also professionally obligated to keep an open mind on the matter. He took copious notes, things to check out. At the end of their meeting, he asked, holding the sugar packet toward her, "Socker. Sugar?"

She smiled, pleased. "Of course, naturaligtvis."

The Chief suppressed an impulse to ask whether **"SO TAB RODER"** meant anything to her.

⋇   *   *   *

One lead the Chief wanted to check out was Olav Klemetsen. Bodil had referred to him as "the crazy Norwegian," a man who had owned a farm near the Swansons'. Olav was now elderly and retired. He lived in the Viking Retirement Home.

Bodil had said that her father and Olav feuded over a range of petty matters over the years, including who should maintain an access road that crossed both their properties as well as fences that divided them. A lot of people had those kinds of differences and did not resort to murder. But differences they were, and perhaps they fed a larger antagonism.

So, he would visit Olav very soon, but before he did, he would call Odin College to ask what **"NO REG"** and **"SO TAB RODER"** meant. Maybe that would produce a lead with which to begin an interview with Olav.

The Scandinavian languages instructor at Odin College puzzled at the words. She could make little of the scrabble, immediately, over the phone. She told him none of the words were Norwegian. Yet one part of the puzzle was Swedish, at least it could be. **"SO TAB RODER"** could be construed as **"SOTA BRODER,"** meaning "sweet brothers." The **"NO REG"** she would have to think about. That didn't offhand sound very promising as a Scandinavian word clue.

Armed with a Swedish phrase, Chief Venzke set off to visit a very elderly Norwegian-American spending his last days in the Viking Nursing Home, owned and run by the Sons of Norway at the edge of Quinlan. The man had been given the sobriquet of "crazy Norwegian," or so Bodil Swanson asserted, by a good number in the community. Beyond that, what impressed the Chief was that one nursing home was Swedish and the other Norwegian. That impression delivered a jolt to him in that he had never made any kind of real distinction between a Norwegian and a Swede, certainly not enough difference in his mind to justify having a separate nursing home for each group. He had heard the names of the nursing homes many times, Viking and

6

Vasa, often in the same sentence, but they had never registered to him as being anything more than interesting Scandinavian names.

Olav, a withered, decaying man, who spoke in a rasp, initially refused to see Venzke. The Chief had to assert his authority as best he could, pointing out to the nursing home director that he was investigating the death of Leonard Swanson. Between the two of them, they made Olav feel that it was incumbent on him to cooperate with such an important investigation. Finally, when the director implied she would withhold his next few meals, Olav consented to a brief interview.

The Chief sat in a straight-back aluminum-and-vinyl chair across from Olav who sat on his bed. After a bit of stylized introductory chitchat, he asked, "What does **SOTA BRODER** mean to you?"

Olav Klemetsen shot back, "It means 'sweet brothers' in Swedish. Everybody knows that."

The Chief looked hard at Olav. "But does it mean anything for the investigation into the death of Leonard Swanson?"

Olav's face twisted with irritation. "I wouldn't know anything about that. Why do you ask such a silly question? Are you taking a Swedish class at Odin College?"

"Not at all. A note with the words **SOTA BRODER** was found near Leonard Swanson's body."

Olav was no help. He responded coolly to a few more questions, then shrugged sullenly, signaling stiffly that the interview had ended.

The Chief decided not to ask about **"NO REG"** until he determined whether it meant anything. He left the Viking Nursing Home feeling keenly that Olav might well know more than he was letting on. His detective's intuition was percolating inside his skull. But why would a Norwegian leave a note in Swedish? It didn't add up, at least not yet. Who were the "sweet brothers"? He needed to know more. To begin, he would try to identify all purchases of Agent Orange in Quinlan in recent weeks. Maybe Olav was among the purchasers.

Yes, Olav had bought the commercial version of Agent Orange in O'Leary's Hardware Store. The store manager remembered the purchase in April, just as the latest snow had been receding into small piles, and spring had begun to seriously arrive, Midwestern style. Over the years, Olav appeared every spring for his herbicides, while he was still farming. But, when he appeared in his late eighties to make such a purchase (after his last previous purchase had been a good five years before, in the spring planting season prior to his retirement), the manager vividly remembered Olav peeling off bills from his trademark roll of cash and lugging a single five-gallon container of Roundup out of the store. It hadn't made sense to him. To make sense of it, he had speculated that it had been a purchase made on behalf of a farming acquaintance, or for a nephew he'd never heard of, or something like that. Certainly he had never heard anything about Olav ever being called "that crazy Norwegian," as Bodil Swanson had alleged. He had never observed or heard about anything crazy in Olav's behavior.

The Scandinavian languages instructor at Odin College called back the next morning. **"NO REG"** was **"NOREG,"** one word, the medieval word for Norway, that the Norwegians were now, with great historic pride, emblazoning on some of their postage stamps, in lieu of the modern word "NORGE."

Chief Venzke sat back in his office armchair. "That's good to know. At least I know it is a word with meaning, a Norwegian word of great significance. But it doesn't seem to do much toward cluing this case together. Do you have more? I need to know about the 'sweet brothers.'"

"Sota broder till tyskarna," came the reply. "That is a phrase that means 'sweet brothers to the Germans' during World War II. Sweden worked hard at staying neutral after the Nazi Army occupied Norway and stayed for five years. The Norwegians were bitter about that for many years."

"Some maybe still are," observed the Chief.

The Chief arranged a meeting with Phyllis Wilkie, the director of the Vasa Nursing Home. He wanted to know if Olav and Leonard had had any recent contact.

Mrs. Wilkie told him that the Vasa and the Viking Nursing Homes had recently enjoyed a party together. Vans from the Viking had transported Olav and others for a dinner and an exchange of gifts at the Vasa. She recalled that Leonard had given Olav a Dalarna horse, a six-inch high, brightly painted wooden horse imported from Sweden's Dalarna Province. In return, Olav had delightedly, though feebly, hugged Leonard and given him his gift. It was a brightly wrapped package of lefse, the traditional, thinly-rolled potato bread of Norway, along with a jar of that Norwegian favorite, cloudberry preserves.

Olav had thanked Leonard profusely and called him affectionately "my fellow Scandinavian." Leonard Swanson had cried tears of joy. He had been deeply moved by Olav Klemetsen's gift.

Olav's arms hung limply as he expired in his room in the Viking Nursing Home. He had eaten a final meal of the same traditional Norwegian lefse spread with cloudberry preserves laced with Agent Orange that he had given his "fellow Scandinavian" Leonard Swanson. Offered as an act of friendship, it was actually an act of revenge for Hitler's invasion of Norway in April, 1940, when Sweden sat neutrally nearby and continued to do so for five agonizing, angering years, dispassionately observing the Norwegians suffer while they, by the standards of that horrible time, prospered, and did only token little for the Norwegians.

Olav had included the mysterious **"NO REG"** note in his gift to Leonard, who had undoubtedly comprehended Olav's meaning as the Agent Orange poisoned him. Olav thought the entire scheme very clever. Only he and Leonard knew. At least that was his plan until Chief Delbert Venzke had visited him.

Now Olav had done what he had to, and, like a good Viking, he had fallen on his sword, at least figuratively so. Some might say he was insane to kill the Swede Swanson, especially so late in life. Others might argue that it was an overdue patriotic act.

Flying Cats

Cats had been flying in the community for several months. It was a mystery. Everyone was baffled.

Jim and Jan Watson were raking leaves in their backyard when a cat fell from the sky. It was one of those cats people were calling "flying cats" and it was dead on impact. Or so they concluded. They had not seen it land. They had only heard it collide with the far corner of their yard. When they went over to investigate, they found it was another of those famous cats they had heard about.

The local newspaper, Quinlan, Iowa's **Quotient**, had published a front-page story on the mysterious cat landings. The title: "Alien Cats? Cats From Outer Space?"

The Watsons had dismissed the newspaper story as the product of excess imagination among the local gossips. Till now.

It was one of those orange "Morris The Finicky Cat" type of cats, if you recall the old TV cat food commercials featuring Morris. This made the landing of the dead cat all the more piercing to Jim and Jan. They loved animals, especially cats. To find a Morris corpse in the yard proved terribly traumatic.

An extraterrestrial cat? That they doubted, but they no longer dismissed the newspaper reports as products of mere rumor. Something serious and bizarre was going on.

It was almost Halloween. Perhaps that had something to do with it. Flying cats instead of flying witches. It was a stretch, but Halloween pranksters never stuck very well to a script. Destructive teens were infamous for their aversion to calendars.

But the cat flying had been going on for months. Likely it had nothing to do with Halloween. The truth probably lay somewhere between aliens and Halloween. Like maybe a sick mind between.

Jan and Jim finished raking the brittle brown leaves that covered their backyard. Carefully, reverentially, they moved the cat's body to the base of a hackberry tree, where it could have a sort of "wake" as they finished cleaning up the yard and pondered what to do.

"I'm stunned about the cat," lamented Jan. "I would have never believed it, had it not happened to us."

Jim made a broad sweep of his arm toward the tall pine fence surrounding their property. "It wasn't our 88-year-old neighbor, Ole, who did it. It wasn't him. He'd never be able to throw a cat high enough to make it look like it landed from the sky."

"But who could it be?" asked Jan. "That cat had to be descending on a pretty steep trajectory. Otherwise, our peripheral vision would have picked it up before it hit."

Jim straightened up from raking and rubbed his chin. "Hmm. That is a fascinating observation." Jim was a high-school history teacher who often made this chin-rubbing gesture and comment.

Jan deposited a rakeful of leaves into a basket. "Something very weird is going on here."

"What are we going to do with the cat?" asked Jim.

"We could call animal control. The city has a man who will pick it up."

"That's for live problem animals, or injured animals. There is no morgue for cats in this town."

"Then we can freeze it. It could be useful evidence once they capture the perpetrator."

"Perpetrator? Suppose there's no perpetrator."

"Don't be silly. Everything has an explanation. There has to be some shenanigans going on here."

"Or extraterrestrial cats invading us."

Jan threw her rake into the air. "Stop joking. This is serious."

Jim cracked a wry smile that seemed downright preternatural.

The cat securely deposited in the basement freezer, the Watsons went upstairs.

Inside the freezer, the cat lay freezing to a hardness beyond rigor mortis. If it were an alien possessed of special powers, there was nothing happening to defy the laws of cryogenics. It was simply a dead cat at the bottom of a freezer in a plastic bag nestled beside a muskie Jim had caught in Wisconsin. If anything were to stir a dead cat out of death, it would be a tasty twelve-pound fish. Yet, nothing happened under the lid of the freezer, except a feline body temperature fast dropping to that of the muskie.

Across the town that afternoon, other cats had landed. One in an alley, another in a front yard shrub, another into the bed of a parked pickup. It was the kind of apparent randomness that engenders the most virulent rumor-mongering. Phones and computers frenetically carried the message that something extraordinary was happening. Stories varied but they were always embellished well beyond the fact that dead cats had been found. One version had it that the cats were witches who had arrived to claim the souls of the minor league baseball team which had ended its season in August with a dismal .115 winning percentage, the worst in league history. Another version had it that cats were falling dead of heart attacks caused by a bad batch of canned cat food delivered to local grocery stores. Perhaps the most outrageous story was that the cats were the sloughed-off bodies of people who were passing on to another reincarnation. All the stories were untrue, but they proved that uncertainty in human events produces an anxiety, if not hysteria, that will work the mind for its most creative fabrications.

The banner headline of the **Quinlan Quotient** read, "Dead Cats Again!" Beneath the banner ran the subhead, "More Than Twenty Found, Origin Unknown." The editor, Ralph Bunning, Jr., had decided that, since no one knew anything yet, he would lay off the alien cat sensationalistic angle this time in favor of

13

more equable reporting. The community nerve endings were too frayed already, maybe beyond short-term repair. He didn't want to contribute toward the unraveling of the community fabric.

Bunning called Police Chief Del Venzke to get an update on the police department's investigation.

"We have not come up with anything yet," reported Venzke. "But we have a man full-time on the case, which is a lot for a small city of 30,000...Something big has got to be behind this. It takes a lot of torque to toss a cat high into the sky."

"What makes you so sure it is a question of torque?"

"Has to be, unless you buy the alien invasion angle. I don't. These were just regular cats, local cats."

"Have you been getting many reports of missing cats?"

"None so far. But we need to get people in here to look at the cats, to see if any belong to them."

"Where are you keeping them?"

"In the freezer in the jail."

"Good idea. Dead cats need to be properly incarcerated."

Venzke hissed at the grisly humor and hung up.

As the chill winds of November tumbled the last of the leaves to the ground, the investigation continued, but all leads proved to be dead ends. In the next few weeks, no massive "day of the flying cats" (the term current in the community) recurred. Only the occasional singleton was found dead, and no finder reported he had heard it thud to the ground. The hysteria and gossip subsided as the high-school football team diverted the attention of the community as it played undefeated ball into the Iowa state championship play-offs. Venzke felt relieved. He couldn't waste any more manpower on those silly cats.

But late one morning, a woman on Waylon Street made a phone call to Chief Venzke to complain about her neighbor. "He keeps working on something in his backyard, even sometimes at two or three in the morning. It looks suspicious to me."

Venzke told the woman he would investigate, just to get rid of her. But later, as he thought about it, he decided to actually look into the matter. He seldom got a call like that that sounded credible. Most conveyed a decidedly fruity quality, which this one clearly did not. Maybe there was something to it. Perhaps something more than the off-hours or eccentric was going on. Maybe looking into it would detect a crime or clear up an unsolved case. As a last possibility, he even thought of the flying cats, as one of several unsolved cases.

Venzke and his deputy, Sid Harmon, went to the front door of the residence on Waylon Street that had been complained about. Harmon stood to one side as Chief Venzke rang the doorbell. They waited a long time and were turning to leave when the door finally opened. A sleepy-eyed, late middle-aged man peered at them. "What can I do for you officers?"

The two men pivoted back toward the door and Venzke said, "Sorry to bother you, but we have a complaint about unusual noises from your backyard, sometimes at two or three a.m. We want to check things out to make sure no one is burglarizing you, for your own safety."

"Unusual noises? From my backyard? Hardly. I would've heard had there been any."

Venzke, himself a community college graduate, noted the erudite construction of the man's sentences. He knew he was talking to an educated man, whether self-taught or formally taught in college. "Can we have a look?" he asked.

The man's tone of voice became defensive. "Certainly not. Out of the question. Sorry."

He began to close the door when Harmon asserted himself. "Sir, wait a minute. What is your name? We have Randolph as the family living here. Is that correct?"

The man nodded. "Yes. I am David Randolph. I work as a security guard at the Big River Nuclear Power Plant. I live alone. Most the time I get home from work early in the morning. Perhaps that explains my neighbor's complaint."

"We didn't mention a neighbor," said Harmon.

"I know that old biddy," said Randolph acidly. "She has nothing better to do than spy on her neighbors."

Chief Venzke gave a conciliatory smile. "Sorry to bother you, Mr. Randolph. I see that you are the victim of a frivolous complaint by a busybody. Please accept our apologies for intruding on your day."

Randolph smiled. "I accept your apology. Have a good day, officers."

Harmon spoke first, once they were back on the road in their squad car. "Another false alarm, Chief."

"Did you see the cat fur on his trousers?"

"He must own a cat."

"Or be a cat killer."

The insurance companies were most interested in solving the "flying cats" mystery. A good number of people were filing insurance claims, and the money claimed had become substantial. For example, one man had filed a claim for his shattered windshield. Another had suffered a broken solarium window and filed a claim. (His wife, he asserted, had suffered a heart attack when the cat had crashed through the window, shattering glass onto her. It fell dead at her feet as she knitted little booties for their one-year-old grandchild.) Yet another had claimed that a cat had put a dent in his home's roof substantial enough to require an entirely new roof. Still another was filing for compensation for post-traumatic stress owing to the shock of a cat landing on his porch.

It is amazing how creative people can become in their claims when an unknown force lurks about. Some had even gone beyond insurance claims to filing lawsuits against whatever entity of government they deemed derelict in not defending the city's air space against flying cats! If only to stop the largely shameless, nonsensical claims and lawsuits, finding the origin of the flying cats would be of great value.

The fallen leaves of November gave way to the icy cold of December. Still the mystery of the flying cats hung over the little city of Quinlan. No cats had flown for over two months and the community trauma had begun to fade in the collective memory. Life had resumed the notoriously dull routine that had made the cats such a welcome respite, a cause celebre that the psyche could wrap hysteria and insurance claims around.

Quinlan was well on its way to returning to being just plain Quinlan. The reporters and camera crews from Chicago, Des Moines, Milwaukee, and even from abroad, including Deutsche Welle, the German TV station, had ceased coming. Because of this, the city council and merchants were not a little sad, for the media had given a nice economic boost to the local economy during their visits, some crews staying a week to ten days, waiting for the next mysterious cat to fly, cameras ready, hoping to videotape a cat in flight and score a media coup. The Quinlan motels and restaurants sorely missed them.

Venzke knew the untoward noise usually occurred about three-thirty a.m., after Randolph had returned home from his shift as a security guard at the Big River Nuclear Power Plant. He learned that Randolph had earned a Ph.D. in history almost thirty years ago, and had never taught college. That amazed him. That somehow made him feel vindicated in his position as police chief, a job with more authority and prestige than Ph.D. Randolph had. He wondered how he had ended up for thirty years in the dead-end position of security guard. It seemed ridiculous that Randolph spent a decade getting a Ph.D. only to spend the next three decades as a security guard.

Could there be a connection between a Ph.D. being a long-term security guard and flying cats? It seemed a farfetched question to ask, but it was important to the stalled investigation to ask improbable questions.

17

Were cats near the nuclear power plant dying of radiation poisoning? Did Randolph dispose of the cats by hurling them about town? If so, how?

Venzke jammed the heel of his palm onto his forehead in a gesture of exasperation. "I should've done it long ago!" he shrilled. "I need to get those cats tested for radiation."

Harmon nodded his agreement. "Long ago," he intoned. "Need to do it."

Venzke had never had any kind of corpse tested for radiation. Where to get the testing done required some sleuthing. Eventually, he was put in touch with Professor Vijay Okaram of the Cornbelt Radiation Laboratory. Dr. Okaram told Venzke that all the frozen cats needed to be transported to the lab, so that the testing could be carried out. There would be no charge as he had to keep occupied some graduate students whose Ph.D. dissertations had foundered but whose grants had not.

In a week, the test results arrived. In a cover letter, Professor Okaram noted, "My students worked hard to provide these radiation test results to you in a timely manner. The assessment of the frozen cats proved a great learning experience for the doctoral students. Should you require assistance in the future, please contact me and advise me of your needs."

The tests showed substantial radiation in all the cats. Now the question became: How did the cats come into contact with the radiation? Was the common link to the lethal radiation one David Randolph? If so, how? Venzke didn't think Vijay would be of any assistance on that issue, though perhaps the levels of radiation reported would help. He scratched his head. "I'll need to talk with the manager of the Big River Nuclear Power Plant," he thought aloud.

Venzke drove along Iowa route 52 to the power plant overlooking the Mississippi River, fifteen miles south of town. He had always felt the government had allowed the plant to be built near Quinlan because it was poorer than Davenport or Dubuque and lacked their political clout. In any nuclear accident, politically impotent Quinlan would be the hardest-hit. Perhaps the dead cats were the bellwether of this victimization, killed by accidentally or illegally leaked radiation that would eventually also kill people.Venzke scratched his head in his typical thoughtful manner. He would have to think about having the next few suspicious deaths in town tested for radiation. He could request tests as part of the autopsies. Likely the radiation in the cats had worked its way up the chain of life, though not yet in sufficient concentrations to kill anyone. Or so he theorized. Police work comprised a lot of theorizing, and he needed to let his mind roam uninhibitedly. The radiation report from Dr. Okaram had proven his thought processes were far from totally speculative.

The summer roadside dazzle of pokeweed, goldenrod, Queen Anne's lace, and purple bergamot had receded into gray brittleness. What had been green, yellow, purple, and vibrant was now skeletal and spiny. On the occasions he had recently walked the roadside, he noted the change in the season by the way the vegetation bristled at him as he brushed by. He took no pleasure in winter. He looked forward to spring and its rejuvenation of the roadside flora that revived his zest for life. Maybe everyone was like him. Or just maybe he suffered some low-order seasonal affective disorder. If so, he could always order some really bright lights at city expense for his office. He also needed to get a check-up soon.

Venzke pulled into the parking lot at the Big River nuke plant. As he hunted for a space, he saw Randolph rounding a corner of the main building. Randolph recognized him and glared.

The Chief glanced at his watch. It was only four p.m. Randolph was not supposed to be here till just before six. Venzke silently cursed himself. He should have made sure he visited the plant when Randolph was away. He had assumed too much. He didn't think Randolph would be around in the afternoon hours at all.

Yet the glare told him far more than his chat with the plant manager did. It told him that his instincts were correct, that he was onto something.

On a whim, the Chief decided to read David Randolph's doctoral dissertation. Once back in his office, he had his secretary fax an order for a copy to University Microfilms on Zeeb Road in Ann Arbor, Michigan.

In a few days, the dissertation arrived. It had been completed and defended for the Ph.D. in History at the University of Iowa in 1969. It was titled "The Medieval Trebuchet In England, 1250-1450." He hunched over the weighty tome, a little intimidated to even open it. It had to weigh at least five pounds. And just what in hell was a "trebuchet"? The word looked very unfamiliar.

Venzke gingerly opened the heavy dissertation, as though the contents might be fragile or even explosive. Ponderously riffling through, he saw that the volume featured a good number of drawings of what he would call catapults. Apparently they were also called trebuchets, pronounced "tray-boosh-shays," and they were used in the wars of the Middle Ages to hurl boulders and molten materials at an enemy. Interesting. And how very practical! No wonder Randolph had been stuck thirty years in a security guard job. Being an expert on trebuchets wouldn't ever get you out of the nuke plant if a college or university didn't hire you. Venzke grimaced. Maybe knowing catapults enabled Randolph to make the Big River nuke plant more secure against assaults from trebuchets. "Hell," he harumphed aloud to himself, as no one was near, "that is why the Big River people had hired Randolph in the first place. He would know how to handle a terrorist trebuchet attack!"

Venzke read on. He soon found that trebuchets did not just hurl boulders and hot melted stuff. They also spread disease among an enemy by hurling dead animals into a fortification, or at least near it. In a time when communicable diseases were not understood, the threat of pestilence from decaying carcasses, risked by people pinned down by bombardment, was very real. The trebuchet had for centuries served as a major instrument of germ warfare.

Bells went off in Venzke's head. Flying cats! Flying cats! Yes, this might be it. Could Randolph be catapulting radioactive cats onto the people and properties of Quinlan? The Chief's mind virtually swelled with excitement in anticipation of cluing together a case against Randolph. He felt a sudden surge of accomplishment. He had used an academic treatise on a hyper-specialized topic to begin to fathom the intellectual background and skills of the possible perpetrator. But what was the motive? He wanted to ask Randolph about that in person.

Venzke had Randolph brought in for questioning. He advised him of his rights and told him he had the right to have an attorney present. He thought Randolph would, if anything, hide behind his rights and drag out the process in the true spirit of a 712-page dissertation on medieval catapults. But that did not happen. Randolph broke down and confessed. It was as if he wanted to get caught. He told all.

Over the years, David Randolph had grown increasingly bitter at never getting an academic position. Confined to his security guard job by a depressed academic market, he did his job joylessly, because he had to. In his spare time, he had managed to publish a couple articles on his dissertation, but these had not catapulted him into academe. Eventually he gave up hope, ceasing to apply for positions. Unfortunately, his thwarted ambition turned to an unhealthy outlet, vengeful on society.

Randolph had taken in cats that strayed near the Big River nuclear plant, fed them, then exposed them to lethal doses of radiation. As a guard, he enjoyed opportunities to perform these executions in the utmost secrecy. Each cat's cadaver was taken home singly in his lunch pail to the freezer in his garage, where they usually accumulated till he had a good supply. He seldom launched just one or two cats.

He fired the cats from his homemade trebuchet hidden among shrubs and trees he had grown into an impressive, vaulting bower just for the purpose of concealing the large wooden, hinged figment of his dissertation. It was the sound the leaves and branches made as the cats flew past that had provided a distinctive rustling sound in Quinlan for months. Without that sound, the neighborhoods nearest the trebuchet just wouldn't be the same.

Meskwaki Burial Mounds

The golf course, set in the most beautiful part of Quinlan, Iowa, in gently rolling hills graced by fir, beech, maple, and weeping willow trees, did not look like a murder scene. But it was. And the suspect was none other than the golf course itself. That was the opinion of the greenskeeper, Ralph Bonte, who over the years had suffered severe migraine headaches and aching joints that he blamed on the course. But at least he was alive. And at least he was paid for his pain. Others weren't so lucky. He'd quit his job if he could afford to. But at his age, 63, with his health problems, who would hire him? Besides, it was a mystery how the golf course killed. He used to think they were just random events, all the misery and death, in and around the links, but now he, and a lot of others, believed strongly that the golf course was the murderer. But how do you arrest a golf course? And if you do, and get a conviction, what is the penalty? 1,000 divots carved out of the heart of its links? Requiring Mike Tyson to play on your fairways and greens as part of his community service? Allow the Chicago Bears to do their summer workouts on the course?

Ralph scratched his head and shrugged. He thought of those who lived near the course who had suffered. Jimmy Zelinski presented perhaps the most poignant portrait of pain. A young boy should never have to go through that.

Jimmy and his parents and sister lived directly across the street from the Quinlan Country Club golf course. One afternoon, the ten-year-old boy came home from school and went straight to the bathroom and projectile-vomited, covering the ceramic tiles and linoleum with a stinking, lumpy blanket. Jimmy was quite sick, and that day would mark the beginning of a terrible decline. It was leukemia.

The authorities finally began to notice Quinlan Country Club. The confusion over which State of Iowa agency had jurisdiction over the golf course had left only semi-investigated for years the health problems of people living near, playing on, or working at the course. Little, ten-year-old Jimmy Zelinski was dying of leukemia and an official from the Iowa Environmental Protection Agency, Winston Singleton, had been belatedly assigned the delicate task of interviewing Jimmy as part of the investigation of the Quinlan Country Club golf course.

Investigator Singleton parked a couple blocks from Jimmy's home. Since he was driving an official State of Iowa agency car, a green sedan with gold logo and lettering, he felt it best if he approached by foot. Parking in front of the Zelinski home somehow reminded him of the scene in the movie **Friendly Fire** where a drab green military sedan pulled up to the Iowa farm home of Peg Mullen, played by actress Carol Burnett, to tell her and her husband that their son had been killed in Vietnam. He was not about to park directly in front of the Zelinski home like that military chaplain and accompanying officer had pulled up to the Mullen farm. That was gross.

Singleton had been investigating the golf course for about two months, studying reports that his agency had compiled and making phone calls and sending e-mails. One thing caught his attention above all else: Everyone who died lived in the homes in the vicinity of the golf course. No one who played golf regularly or worked at the country club had died. They suffered a lot of discomfort, especially horrendous headaches and aching joints, but none had gotten life-threateningly ill. It was an anomaly that had set his mental machinery awhir, so far with no answer.

As he walked past the neat, well-tended, modest homes that lined the street facing the back nine of the course, Singleton felt a little pang stab at him. He would have had a hard time expressing it in words, but it derived from the total injustice of a young boy dying before he had reached one-fifth of Singleton's age. In his agency, he hadn't had to confront death much, like the highway patrol and the Department of Criminal Investigation did. He had seen a lot of dead fish, maybe millions, and a smattering of dead raccoons and deer. (Yes, Iowa has a lot of deer living at the fringes of the corn and in and near its city parks and residential areas.) And a good number of people had become sick from the effluvia of hog lots spilling into their water supply. But environmental investigation had never taken him before to a dying ten-year-old boy.

Singleton sniffed the air and breathed in deeply. For a bright May day, the air tasted and smelled flat and stale. There was no particular odor, but the absence of the sharp freshness of all that had leafed out and flowered, struck him as distinctly odd. That reinforced his active sense of the injustice and cosmic sadness of a young boy facing death.

Mrs. Zelinski answered the doorbell and let Singleton in. She knew he'd arrive at three p.m., and was dressed semi-formally in a blue suit, lavender scarf, and navy blue pumps. Seldom did Singleton experience an interviewee who accorded him enough importance to so dress. Mr. Zelinski was still at work, which was fine with him. Often, too much family impeded an interview. And this was a delicate one. He hoped to finish before the tears started to copiously flow. He wanted to emotionally distance himself. He had a job and his mental health to protect.

The Zelinski living room featured a Persian-style carpet arranged over gray carpeting. The furniture was also subdued with accents added on: a pair of pale green armchairs with colorful antimacassars and a pale-green matching sofa with a Mexican-looking serape-type thing draped over the middle of it. Either the Zelinskis traveled or they had been to K-Mart. Probably K-Mart, opined Singleton to himself, because the stuff looked like it had been made in Thailand.

Singleton sat in one chair and Mrs. Zelinski sat in the other, separated by an oblong mahogany-veneered fruitwood coffee table. He set his notepad on the table and began his interview. "When do I get to see Jimmy?" (By e-mail, Mrs. Zelinski had

25

advised him that Jimmy had his good and bad days, and if three p.m. Thursday proved part of a bad day, only she, not Jimmy, would be able to respond to his questions.)

"Jimmy is having a very bad day," she intoned. "It's the chemo. Sometimes it really puts him down, like today." She looked down at the table, fixing on it briefly. "I'm afraid he won't be able to talk with you. He was looking forward to it. He doesn't have many visitors these days."

"I understand." He paused, poising his pen over the notepad. "Could you tell me how your life in this house has been affected by the golf course? Feel free to say whatever comes to mind."

Mrs. Zelinski shifted forward in her chair, planting her feet like pillars. "It stinks a lot sometimes. But I can't for sure blame the golf course for that. It's kind of a mystery."

"What's mysterious about it?"

"The smell never comes till very late at night."

"Like about what time?"

"Well, like when we're in bed and in deep sleep. It's hard to keep track of anything during that time of night."

Singleton nodded. "So you think something happens in the wee hours. Something with a malevolent smell."

"Something, but I couldn't say it came from the golf course. If it came from the course, you'd think it'd be smelly all the time, wouldn't you?"

"You would think that. That's what I want to find out."

The interview went on for about an hour. When Singleton heard the cuckoo clock in the living room announce intrusively that four p.m. had arrived, he drew his chat with Mrs. Zelinski to a polite close, wishing her and her son the best. "I may talk with Jimmy later?" he finished. She said that would be OK on one of Jimmy's good days, when he could come out of his bedroom and talk.

Singleton suggested that a phone call might be the best way to enable Jimmy to talk during a good hour. "That way we won't have to rely on the luck of the day." He put his hat on and tipped it toward her. "Good day, until we meet again."

Mrs. Zelinski smiled thinly and escorted him out.

The next day, Singleton met with Ralph Bonte at the Quinlan Country Club. They sat at a corner table in the very finely appointed restaurant and ordered. Ralph had baked Hawaiian mahi and Singleton had an Iowa pork steak with a special piquant house sauce, both meals ordered on his expense account. (Mrs. Singleton was a gourmet cook and he intended to ask the club chef for the sauce recipe. It rivaled a sauce he and his wife had delighted in at a Stockholm five-star restaurant, the Gota Canal, on a Scandinavian trip several years ago.) About halfway into their meal, Singleton broached the subject of the golf-course-as-killer.

He put down his fork and eyed Bonte seriously. "I read in the reports that you've had your health problems since you've worked here."

Bonte nodded. "It's the damndest thing. I took early retirement from Quinlan Corn and Soy and I take this job. Less pay, but I'm drawing a pension, and this is in a beautiful setting. It looked like paradise compared to the QC & S factory. One hundred and ten degrees inside in summer, and whatever the temperature is outside in winter, adjusting a little for the body heat from the employees." Bonte gave a bitter laugh. "That's what I get for dropping out of high school." He shrugged. "I guess for what I have to offer the world, I did OK."

Singleton smiled comfortingly. "So you think this 'beautiful setting' is not the paradise you once thought it would be?"

Bonte shifted in his chair, briefly glancing out the window toward the links. "For sure. Every morning I get up, I'm stiff beyond my years. It takes longer and longer every year to limber up and get to work. And it's not something the doctors can put a finger on. I've taken every kind of test they got, and they haven't learned anything for certain yet. All they have are suspicions."

"Which are?"

"You know, the same-o, same-o, that the golf course has something to do with it." Bonte's face hardened. "That course is some kind of monster that maims and kills. There's some kind of poltergeist in it or something. I think it is the spirits."

"Spirits?"

"Yes, the spirits of dead Meskwaki Indians. They had a lot of burial mounds here before the golf course went in. There was a big controversy about it before they started putting it in. Lots of protests by tribal members who came from far and wide to join the few area tribal members. That was over 25 years ago."

Singleton looked astounded. "The Indians weren't mentioned in any of the reports. I thought I was dealing with a possible environmental problem here, not a matter of spirits."

Bonte furrowed his brow. "I don't know what you're dealing with. All I know is that nothing else seems to explain it, so why not consider the burial mounds that were once here. The bulldozers leveled them so white men can clobber little white balls here and there. Does that sound sinful, or what?"

"I think I need to get in contact with the Meskwaki leaders," observed Singleton. "Could you give me a name?"

"Jonathan Leading Wolf. He's the one leader of the Meskwaki who lives in Quinlan. He kind of speaks for them here on the local level."

Singleton hadn't expected to be interviewing a Meskwaki leader, but here he was knocking on Jonathan Leading Wolf's door. Isn't investigating interesting? he was thinking as Jonathan opened the door. "I've been expecting you. Come on in," Leading Wolf said in a montone.

As Singleton gave the living room a cursory looking over, he wondered where all the casino profits of the Meskwaki had gone. There was certainly no evidence here of them in the pinched, drab, but authentically Meskwaki room. Paint was peeling from the walls and ceiling. The furniture was third-user-Salvation

Army. And the carpet needed to be removed as a public health measure. Yet, the red catlinite pipe on a small table, flanked by eagle feathers, twists of brown-and-black tobacco, and a dreamcatcher nailed unartistically to a wall with an eight-penny nail (where a brad nail would have sufficed) spoke to the Native American identity of Jonathan Leading Wolf in a stark, compelling way. A book of poems by Meskwaki poet Ray Young Bear lay opened to a poem entitled "The Significance Of A Water Animal," further testimony to the tribal consciousness that dominated the décor.

Jonathan popped open two beers, setting one down in front of Singleton. He gulped from his can as he sat down. Singleton felt he'd better drink too. He took a tentative swig. The several empty beer cans scattered about the room were certainly not Meskwaki artifacts. Singleton surmised he had arrived well into a serious drinker's afternoon's drinking. He was struck with the ease with which he had been included in the drinking. He'd read an article in an anthropology class years ago about "companionate drinking" among certain tribes, how drinking was a major way for them to socialize, to bond, and how their imbibing had an enveloping cultural significance. The article had claimed that only white men liked to drink alone. He felt a surge of satisfaction in recalling that article from a required liberal arts class that he detested then as useless but had just applied in a pragmatic way, nearly thirty years after he had squeezed by with a C-. Jonathan Leading Wolf had just brought him into the cultural fold for the afternoon. He was Jonathan's "functional companion," there being apparently no authentic options available. Singleton felt honored.

"I'm glad you invited me over," began Singleton. "I feel lucky to get to see you on short notice."

Leading Wolf leaned back in his chair. "I'm always ready to talk about my tribe. We want to keep our culture alive."

"I'm told that you are a tribal leader. What position do you hold?"

29

Leading Wolf laughed, waving his arm over the living room. "As you can see, I'm not a representative of the Meskwaki Casino. I don't know where the big profits go, though I get a small monthly check. I think the big money gets siphoned off by the white consultants the tribal council hires." He paused. "But to answer your question, I am a shaman. I keep the old religious rituals and practices alive."

"Did you perform rituals at the burial mounds where the Quinlan Country Club now stands?"

"Many, many times. It tore me apart to see that golf course go in. Our tribe will never be the same. The spirits of our ancestors will never rest in peace until their bones are taken out of the museums and buried there again. It gives the Meskwaki great pain to see what has happened, to experience this bad treatment of us."

Singleton nodded sympathetically. "There are laws now to prevent this sort of thing from happening, aren't there?"

"Yes, and casino money is being donated to politicians who will enforce the laws and make sure it does not happen again. But when that golf course went in over twenty-five years ago, there was no stopping them. We protested, but they just threw us all in jail from a few days to a few months. I got the worst, a full year in the county jail, so that I'd really get their message, that golf was the most important religion in Quinlan."

"I see," said Singleton, almost reflexively, rubbing his chin in a thoughtful-nervous gesture. "Well, let's take the golf course today. Do you have any kind of take on what causes all the cancer and other illnesses among residents living near the Quinlan Country Club."

Leading Wolf ran a finger over the turquoise in the silver buckle of his cowboy-style belt. "The spirits are angry. The whites have savaged our graves. So, whites are dying."

"As a Meskwaki shaman, you can help me get to the bottom of this. Could you assist me?"

Jonathan Leading Wolf nodded.

In the wee hours of the morning, Ralph Bonte, Jonathan Leading Wolf, and Winston Singleton exited the clubhouse overlooking the golf course. Singleton led the way. He'd called the local police department to let them know he was doing some necessary nocturnal sleuthing so that no squad cars would suddenly appear with patrolmen brandishing their .38s.

If what Mrs. Zelinski had told him had any validity, Singleton figured it was worth the effort to get Leading Wolf onto the links about three a.m., to see what his shamanistic powers might detect. He did not tell his superiors what he was doing. They would think him hare-brained and order him to stop. But, since he was working off the clock, as they say in retail sales, he decided that this was none of their business, only his personal experiment in the investigative potential of Meskwaki shamanism.

The three of them quartered the links systematically, seeking to cover it in its entirety. Singleton had no idea what to expect. He had laid his investigation into the hands of a shaman for a few hours in what he regarded as a kind of act of faith, or at least a brief suspension of his intermittent pew-warming Presbyterian faith.

A half-moon helped the three negotiate the links, assisted by street lights along the street in the near distance. Leading Wolf observed in a low tone, without going into an explanation, how it was indeed a very good night for a Meskwaki shaman to be out on the greens and fairways, flanked by silhouettes of glorious weeping willow trees. How magnificent the trees were!

Leading Wolf led them, and eventually, after a lot of quartering the links, they came to the brook that ran along the eastern edge of the course. It wasn't much, no more than three to four inches deep, a nice accent to the nature-scene effect that designers of such courses like to achieve.

Leading Wolf stood silently at the brook. But soon he fell back, because the water began to rise. It rose quickly, doubling or tripling the volume of the creek in a matter of minutes. And as

31

the water rose, a horrendous stench rose with it. A kind of horrific smelly mist curled up from the creek, spreading over the lower-lying parts of the golf course. It soon got so dense that none of them could see the moon or the street lights. Their eyes began to swell with tears and they became nauseous.

The heavy mist, much like a fog bank, spread toward the nearby homes, one of which was home to Jimmy Zelinski. Singleton felt he was witnessing, and suffering, the source of whatever caused Jimmy's cancer. But what was it? He tapped Leading Wolf on the shoulder and asked, "What do you think?"

Leading Wolf did not answer. His eyes narrowed and his face squinched up against the smell as he began reverentially to chant something in Meskwaki. He pulled out a twist of tobacco, and shredded it into the creek. Then he dipped his hands into the water to finish the ritual. He cried out, as part of the ritual, Singleton thought. But when Leading Wolf extracted his hands from the creek, they were painfully blistered.

Bonte and Singleton got him quickly back to the club house for first aid treatment.

Singleton left Ralph to attend to Leading Wolf. He walked upstream, going a couple miles into a stand of young willow trees that opened into an upscale tract of split-level homes in the half-million to million-dollar price range. He continued past the tract, unnerved by a barking dog as he moved, but no one became alarmed. At least no lights he could see came on.

Past the fancy subdivision, the smell and high water in the stream disappeared. Singleton hypothesized that the source of all the problems of the past few years associated with the golf course lay somewhere amid those beautiful homes owned by some of the richest people in Quinlan.

Singleton retreated to the clubhouse before the sun could rise.

Singleton and his agency monitored the creek over the next few nights. Not every three a.m., but most, the little creek rose.

They collected samples for analysis. Each night that it rose brought basically the same cocktail of toxic chemicals. They were, for the most part, toxic chemicals as well as industrial solvents and additives requiring a permit to dispose in a carefully prescribed way at a state-licensed facility. Clearly, someone had been illegally dumping toxic waste into the stream that flowed into and along the golf course. Who, and for how many years, Singleton wanted to determine in the worst possible way.

Weeks of investigation produced a lead. One Arthur Marger, who lived in one of the fancy homes upstream, had been denied access to dispose of toxic waste at state facilities nine years earlier. His license had been revoked for toxic waste violations. The State of Iowa also fined him heavily. They wanted him out of the toxic waste disposal business.

However, the State had never notified the corporations that Marger's license had been revoked and it did not monitor where all the chemical waste from companies was going in a coordinated fashion among its agencies. This provided Arthur Marger a niche for a resurgent corporate toxic waste business, from which he made a good income. Regularly, he dumped his clients' barrels of waste into large plastic pipes that ran underground from inside his garage to points at the bottom of the stream that ran along the golf course. He had been doing this for over nine years.

Jonathan Leading Wolf believed firmly that, had it not been for the golf course displacing the Meskwaki ancestral graves, an evil spirit in the form of Arthur Marger would never have poisoned the sacred creek of his tribe.

As for Arthur Marger, the State made a felon of him and sentenced him to twenty years at the Ford Dodge Penitentiary in north-central Iowa. There, he drew the spring and summer assignment of helping to tend an organic garden, where no pesticides or herbicides are applied. However, some of his fellow inmates manage to regularly put into his meals small amounts of chemicals that they steal from the prison paint shop. Not too much, just enough to keep him feeling the pain of a ten-year-old kid undergoing chemotherapy.

Jimmy Zelinski died two months later.

Hog Scent #30

"It smells like hog shit!" cried Bill Hall, as he and his wife Laurie cruised the old Lincoln Trail Highway, now called Highway 30, in central Iowa. The Lincoln Trail, at ten-year intervals, is resurrected in memory as auto buffs nostalgically travel cross-country the first highway to stretch from the Atlantic to the Pacific. But there was no nostalgia that day for Bill and Laurie. Only a terrible smell that assailed their olfactory senses in the most horrific way, making them nauseous.

Closing the windows on their '88 Olds only compounded their misery on a hot, muggy day. The air conditioning, which would have offered some relief, had gone on the fritz the day before. Today was Sunday and Monday was the earliest the Halls could get their car to an auto repair shop, if they were lucky.

"This is the most vile smell I've ever experienced," said Laurie, her nose squinched up in revulsion, her heat-stressed face seeming a bit demonic. The hot stinky air poured through the open windows, swirling about, impregnating them with the odor. Fresh from attending the service at St. Olav Lutheran Church in Quinlan, they were becoming rapidly frazzled. Their Sunday-best clothes would have to be dropped off at the dry cleaner's before they left the car for air conditioner repair. The Lutheran minister, Reverend Larsen, a young man who usually dwelt on upbeat themes in his sermons, had that morning sermonized on the Lutheran concept of hell. And then he had sent them off straight into it!

"This is intolerable," complained Bill, loosening the tie on his summer dress shirt. "This is not normal hog farming."

The gently rolling land spread out before them on either side of Highway 30. But instead of the bucolic Grant Wood view of tall corn and rambling farm houses big enough to raise a dozen kids to perfection that made even big-city people who had never

35

known farm life vaguely homesick, what unfolded before them was a huge corporate hog farm, a kind of Hog Auschwitz for thousands and thousands of hogs.

The humid air carried palpably the intense, heavy smell of hog excrement, what Bill was quick to label "Hog Scent #30," in an anti-nostalgia fit of pique directed at the old Lincoln Highway. The highway now offered an environmental hazard, a far contrast from the fond memories of a bygone era.

The Halls drove home, angry and getting angrier. Traditionally, rural Iowans stoically endure what travesties and tragedies come their way, bolstered by their faith in God. A Lutheran God had proved especially useful in enlarging the capacity of Iowans to endure. But times had changed. Many of them were now on the Internet, part of the global community that valued instant gratification. The Halls were not about to suffer silently.

By the time they glided into the driveway of their frame home with new aluminum siding, in the tiny country village of Prescott, population 380, they had become angry enough to be hog-tied in order to constrain their furor. Less than an hour earlier, they had sung Martin Luther's "A Mighty Fortress Is Our God." So they felt especially empowered to try to do something about the hell they had just experienced. Rev. Larsen, after all, had preached that a good deal of hell on earth is man-made and could thus be changed. There was also the other part of it, he had pontificated, that was due to a person being an object as well as an actor, being very vulnerable flesh and bones as well as having a tremendous capacity to act, magnified by a vast array of technology, to alter his or her own destiny. The Reverend had gotten a bit too abstrusely theological for them both on that. Yet they had gotten the gist of his message.

Bill Hall taught seventh grade in Quinlan, population about 30,000. He and Laurie lived a thirty-minute drive away because they loved country living. They had been married a year and intended to soon start a family. They envisioned a childhood for their baby in Prescott featuring very little noise and traffic, no crime and gangs, and fresh air. The last of their trilogy of requirements had suddenly been put at risk.

They had not been unaware of the huge hog lots, also called "hog confinements" or "hog factories." They regularly read the **Quinlan Quotient** about this new form of economic development that would help sustain and augment Iowa's prosperity. They could only approve, for the paper presented it in glowing, win-win terms. Now they had grave doubts.

After school Monday, Bill picked up his repaired car and drove to a four p.m. appointment with the Quinlan County Attorney, Mickey Mead.

The county building rose five stories, a yellow quarried limestone pile built near the turn of the century, rehabbed several times, big rooms divided and redivided and divided again to accommodate the several government activities that bulged against its walls.

Bill had no problem finding a parking spot in the late afternoon in a lot that during most of the day was crammed. He was pleased that the air conditioning in his car now worked superbly against the hot, humid day. Although he remained plenty provoked at one hog lot in particular and all of them in general, he entered the building in a slightly better mood than his totally black one on Sunday.

Bill did not wait long in the waiting room. The County Attorney was on schedule with his appointments, and his secretary escorted Bill into his office. Mead, a huge monolith of a man, wore a blue summer dress shirt, cherry-red tie, and charcoal dress slacks. He smiled broadly beneath a broad mustache as he shook Bill's hand. "So, it's about the big hog lot between here and Prescott," he smiled.

Bill nodded. He recounted what he and Laurie had experienced Sunday. Mead seemed very sympathetic. "These hog factories look more like a mixed blessing now that they've gotten in here. They should've stayed in North Carolina." Mead parted his hands expansively toward Bill, to dramatize his words. "Those Tar Heels may need the big hog lot business, but we Hawkeyes aren't so desperately poor that we have to suffer it."

Mead dropped his hands. Bill thought he sounded like a true politician the way he ingratiated himself over the issue.

"There is a bit of a jurisdictional issue here," continued Mead. "The environmental people in Des Moines may be the most appropriate for this. But I'll have the Sheriff check it out now. There might be some sort of county violation we can tag them with. At least your complaint gives us a reason to go out and have a look."

Bill smiled. "I appreciate it."

Sheriff Sid Dunleavy laid the phone receiver back onto its cradle. He had just talked with County Attorney Mead, who had requested that he visit the hog lot on Highway 30. The thought of going onto the premises where thousands of hogs were fed till they were slaughtered was not his idea of a fun outing. He'd almost rather deal with another methamphetamine case, and there were sure a lot of those lately. But, variety is the spice of life, or maybe smell would be a better term, he thought, as he put on his hat and left the office.

The Sheriff and his deputy, Chris Powell, took the main drag out of town, Quinlan Street, a road flanked by industries. The small city was a regional manufacturing and processing center. Along this road, smell was often the preeminent reality, especially on hot, humid, windless days. South Quinlan's poor neighborhoods suffered mightily on those days. Smell was a measure of progress; the more smelly a city, the more prosperous, at least for the affluent neighborhoods. He tipped back his hat as he watched recede in the rearview mirror East Iowa Manufacturing, Hawkeye Highwater Pumps, and other smokestack enterprises emitting spirals of foul pollution.

He glanced toward Powell who was popping jelly beans from a small plastic bag into his mouth, chewing slowly. "You've driven by American Heartland's hog lot. What did you notice?"

Powell gulped down a jelly bean in order to answer. In a few seconds the answer emerged from his throat. "I've driven by that hog lot many times, but hardly ever does a smell from there bother me. It's odd how that happens, how sometimes it stinks and how sometimes it doesn't. Must be the weather, or something like that, that makes the place stink once in a while."

"Plus the hog crap," interjected the Sheriff. "Without that, there's nothing to warm up to make the stench."

Powell threw his head back and laughed heartily. The Sheriff couldn't see how his words could be that funny, or even funny at all.

The day had an eery feeling to it, like something out of the ordinary was about to happen, mused the Sheriff. Was it the heat that threatened to fry his brain that made him so full of foreboding? Or was it a lawman's sense of the future, that intuition that enables him to prosecute evil while evading it himself? The fields of soy and corn, bounded by hedgerows, dotted with farms and their houses and utility buildings, whisked by as he drove. It was as if those fields and buildings sweeping by were taking him to some place he'd rather not be. Oh, what the hell, he grimaced, as he suffered the jelly bean chewing sounds of Powell. It was probably that he had been Sheriff so long that the cumulation of all the little and big stresses had become a generalized anxiety. Maybe he had taken one too many of those in-service workshops on police stress and had become too sensitive to everything.

The Sheriff swung the cruiser onto Highway 30 from Quinlan Street. He tried to focus his mind on the task at hand, a visit to the American Heartland Hog Factory. He had read they handled up to 50,000 hogs at a time. Now that is stress! He relaxed his grip on the steering wheel. That sort of put things into perspective.

The Sheriff had been reading up on agriculture lately, mostly by going through the **Farm and Country** section of the Sunday paper. He had noted (he may have learned it in high school but forgotten) that Iowa had not always been a corn state. In its early days there was little corn. Raising cattle and clearing marsh in order to plant vegetable gardens and a plot of corn for a family had predominated. Hybrid corn, especially high-yield "dent corn," was developed and it transformed the land into an ocean of corn that was grown by family farmers for decades. But, in recent decades, the small farms had been disappearing, absorbed by larger farms and corporate conglomerates. Hog farms, by contrast, had been until very recently family-run and small in scale. Yet, their turn to be challenged by bigness had arrived. Corporate hog farming was transforming the countryside with the establishment of huge hog factories that were putting family hog operations out of business. For both corn and hogs, bigness reigned supreme.

Powell folded his bag of jelly beans shut. He had polished off half of them, with one just tossed onto his tongue. He wanted to save the remaining half for the return trip to headquarters. He had graduated from Quinlan High six years before and gone on to community college, earning an A.A. degree. For a couple years after his degree, he had done construction work, mostly in Iowa and Illinois. Growing tired of that line of work, he joined the Quinlan County Sheriff's Department two years ago. He had sailed through the Iowa Sheriffs' Institute three-month course near Cedar Rapids as well as his six-month probationary period. He now felt secure and relaxed enough to eat jelly beans in squad cars. Along with his wife, baby son, hunting, fishing, jetskiing, and drinking beer, jelly beans ranked right up there among life's pleasures.

"There she is," observed Powell as the American Heartland Hog Factory appeared in view. "Isn't she a beaut?"

Powell had a sense of humor and the Sheriff found him more pleasant to team up with than many in the department. "Yeah, the American Beauty Rose," he returned, smiling thinly.

The hog factory sprawled, a complex of corrugated aluminum buildings. It exuded palpable evil, structures of horror, representing the killing of one species so another could grow fat. Vegetarians proclaimed this kind of assessment, mused the Sheriff. Pigs were farrowed here, fed to maturity, and slaughtered for market as hogs. What economists call "economy of scale" made it a very profitable venture. Yet it was still evil, a business of killing for profit.

Powell sniffed the air. He smelled nothing comparable to the horrific smell that Bill Hall had reported. Neither did the Sheriff.

They parked outside the manager's office and got out, alighting on a thick swath of gravel that served as a small parking lot. The wind was picking up and fluffy clouds could be seen in the distance, to the southwest. Powell swallowed the last remnant of a purple jelly bean.

The hog lot manager, Steve Winship, a portly man who wore size fourteen shoes, waddled to the door to let the Sheriff and Powell in. He offered an unctuous smile, intended to disarm rather than convey pleasure in receiving the two men. He was, to be blunt, the perfect manager of a hog lot. He even looked about as much like a hog as a human being can be and still be physically up to performing the duties of his position. The Sheriff and Powell felt an immediate sense of discomfort around Winship.

"How can I help you?" asked Winship.

"We don't want to make too big a thing of what may be a small thing," said the Sheriff. "But we've had a complaint about a horrific odor from this place, so bad that it stings the eyes and causes nausea."

Winship wrinkled his brow contemplatively, organizing his thoughts deliberately. He had climbed the corporate ladder a bit to a nice manager's job in part because he avoided shoot-from-

41

the-hip responses that he might regret. He had also learned to answer questions vaguely with lots of escape hatches built into artfully oblique answers. "I will be very pleased to discuss the issue with you. The American Heartland Hog Factory wants to be accessible, to be transparent, to participate in the democratic process."

Powell thought he might throw up. The Sheriff wasn't about to do that, but he could see that Winship was indeed a greasy creature, probably a product of the University of Iowa's MBA program with a major in Agri-Business. "We're happy about that," smiled the Sheriff. "It's nice to have a fine, upstanding corporate citizen here in Quinlan County. We could use a lot more like you."

"I can show you the layout of this hog factory if you'll accompany me into the office. We have a color-coded map on the wall to show visitors, to give them an idea of the operation."

The Sheriff and Powell followed Winship into his office, a big one, with large desk, computer, fax machine, and file cabinets on one side. The other side offered a scale model of the hog operation. A large map (sort of a blueprint in red, green, yellow, and blue) took up a good chunk of the wall behind the model, about a four-feet-by-six space. The royal blue wall-to-wall carpet had that new-carpet feel underfoot, and it emitted an enticing, almost perfumy scent. The Sheriff guessed that the carpet had been treated to do just that, to mask what Bill Hall had irately termed "hog scent #30."

Once inside, Winship stood in the center of the office and invited the attention of the Sheriff and Powell to the map. He explained where the various operations of the hog lot took place, using a laser pointer as he talked. The corporate logo, a gold silhouette of a very fat hog, arced over the colorful map of the facility. The company's name, in gold letters a half-foot high, **The American Heartland Hog Factory**, ran horizontally below the logo and above the map. A model of the facility, standing on a long plywood table, offered great detail, including miniature hogs and people, conferring a sense of activity to the highly crafted display. The entire exhibit, a tremendous PR effort, aimed to please.

Winship's gushing presentation about the virtues of the hog lot went on about an hour. At the beginning, it was informational and direct. About halfway through, it began to get outright boring. Neither the Sheriff nor Powell could see why Winship would want to lecture an "audience" of just two so lengthily. It simply didn't make any sense, or at least it didn't until the presentation began to wind down. It was approaching 5:30 p.m., far past quitting time. Perhaps what they were enduring was a filibuster of their very presence.

Winship brought his lecture to a close. "Hog products, sirs, that is the future of our region. The more product, the more prosperity here. And we at American Heartland are capable of creating prosperity with our large production capacity." He turned his back to his "audience" and walked to his desk, picking up his jacket and hat. "Quitting time," he smiled.

"But don't we get a tour of the facility?" exclaimed the Sheriff.

"Sorry gentlemen. This is the only tour we give. We simply don't want the poor PR and increased insurance risk that comes with lots of people traipsing through our hog lot. It is simply not the kind of facility that you tour. That is why they have me here. Not only to manage the facility, but to give people like you a guided tour via lecture and map." He straightened his tie self-importantly. "I hope you're satisfied because that's the best we can do for you."

The Sheriff spoke in a very irritated tone. "But we need to look into a smell problem here. Remember, we have a citizen's complaint about a horrific problem here."

Winship quipped, repeating an old adage, "Each to his own taste said the old man as he kissed the cow." He paused, simpering. "I guess I really should say hog."

43

The Sheriff bridled at the jest, brushing aside a strand of hair that had strayed over his right eye. "We'll be back with a search warrant if we have to," he challenged.

"Search for what? Hog manure?" retorted Winship. "Do you realize how ridiculous such a search warrant would be? No judge will sign it."

"We'll see about that," returned the Sheriff, who beckoned to Powell with a crisply flung hand, motioning toward the squad car that they were leaving.

The car glistened in the early evening sun as it traveled the access road from the manager's office to Highway 30. Both officers thought it odd that there was no pungent hog smell that could rate the sobriquet, "Hog Scent #30." There was only your basic barnyard hog smell. Nothing unusual. This, plus the fob-off they just endured, made for a serious mystery at American Heartland. There must be an explanation. Some sleuthing would be necessary.

The next morning, the Sheriff and Powell reported back to County Attorney Mead. Mead's frame was as extended as it could be in his executive swivel armchair, his feet on his desk. He snapped his galluses softly, rhythmically, as he listened to the Sheriff report. Mead knew how to relax his body, semi-siesta style, throughout a long humid Iowa day. He was unlikely to ever die of a heart attack, the Sheriff thought. But pressure sores and the attendant infections might eventually bring him down.

A ceiling fan rotated, slightly wobbly, emitting a repetitive click-click, not quite enough to be irritating, but noticeable. Mead had positioned a folded handkerchief on his chest, in case talking caused his face to perspire. He was particular like that. Everything consisted of a risk for which a solution must be readied, or, better yet, a way found to avoid the risk entirely. That was his life's pre-eminent strategy. He must have maintenance adjust the click-click out of that fan before the day

was over. Not fixing it risked disrupting the routines of himself and his staff.

The Sheriff recounted the experience at American Heartland, shifting in his chair with every sentence in his clinging, freshly pressed uniform. He wondered what his wife had sprayed on his threads before she ironed, or just exactly what she had done. The itching and clinging distracted him sufficiently so that he had to concentrate a little more than usual on what he was saying. Beside him, Powell sat ramrod upright, his hands clasped over his jelly-bean paunch.

"We had a very odd experience out there at American Heartland," the Sheriff began. "Their manager, Winship, filibustered us over an hour. Then he dismissed us. Said he wouldn't even think of giving us a tour of their hog factory. I told him I might be back with a search warrant."

Powell interjected, "He laughed when the Sheriff mentioned a warrant. 'Search for what?' he said."

The County Attorney puckered his brow thoughtfully, giving his galluses a couple of half-hearted snaps, a kind of grace note to the languid rhythm of his gently rocking in his swivel chair. "Sounds devious. Smells fishy."

"Smells like manure," corrected Powell.

The County Attorney nodded, slightly taken aback, corrected by a factotum on the nether end of the criminal justice hierarchy. "Winship obviously doesn't want you looking around, making your own conclusions. He wants to tell you what the place is about. That looks devious to me."

The Sheriff scooted forward in his chair. "Can we get a search warrant?"

"I think Judge Patterson will grant us one. I've had my secretary type up the substance of Bill Hall's complaint. That ought to get us a warrant." He paused meaningfully. "Stinking up Highway 30 can be classified as some sort of environmental crime or at least a public nuisance. We should be able to go in and take a look on the basis of that."

Powell wished in the worst way he could finagle one of the jelly beans out of his pocket and get it to his lips. But he didn't want to risk offending those on the hierarchy above him. Perhaps, when he had a few more years in, he would feel comfortable eating his favorite candy in their presence. He looked forward to that day! Right now, all he could do was sit erect and pay close attention. He wanted to help resolve the riddle that the hog factory presented. He exchanged looks with the Sheriff.

"Anything to add?" the Sheriff asked.

Powell pursed his lips, emitting a subtle smack. "I hope I can be part of the search warrant team. This situation out there is like a puzzle that needs piecing together. I like puzzles."

The Sheriff smiled. "If and when we get the warrant, you and I'll execute it together."

Mead amended, "When you get the warrant."

The Sheriff shifted in his chair and smiled. Powell made ready to exit. His goal: a jelly bean, a luscious purple one.

Armed with the warrant, the Sheriff and Powell drove toward a second encounter with the big hog factory that sprawled over a thousand acres of rich prairie earth, the best soil in the world in which to introduce a seed and watch it thrive to maturity. What a waste, farming hogs on the precious God-given sod of Iowa, reflected the Sheriff acidly. Why, any soil would do for hogs! No one needed the world's best soil to produce pork chops and ham.

The Sheriff gave the accelerator a little nudge. An anger toward Winship and the hog factory rose in him. As a kid, he had learned to be wary of big corporations from his father, who worked as a mechanic in the Iowa Midland Railroad's roundhouse and was a good exemplar of the pro-union, suspicious-of-big-business attitude of many railroad employees. He had, by achieving success a bit beyond his expectations, becoming Sheriff, set aside much of this attitudinal baggage. But

now he felt a little of it being loaded back onto him by some ethereal porter, who looked a lot like his late father.

This time they had not called ahead. They meant to forcibly, if necessary, examine the premises of a mysterious hog lot that sometimes stank a lot, sometimes smelled hardly at all. Hogs cannot avoid smelling, even if they eat from troughs of feed laced with Chanel perfume.

Not a farm kid himself, the Sheriff felt a surge of anticipation, despite his initial revulsion to the idea of a visit to the hog lot. This was the first hog farm he had ever set foot on, or at least it was his second visit to his first one. People outside Iowa cannot understand that Iowa town kids were about as unlikely as town kids anywhere to set foot on a farm, especially a mega-hog farm. Amazingly, this was as big an adventure to him as visiting Masai cattle herders in Kenya, which he had done on a trip sponsored by his church three years ago.

They pulled up at the manager's office. The place had an "OPEN" sign up, but looked unoccupied. No lights were on inside, at least none they could see.

The Sheriff felt a little relieved. He'd just as soon not deal with that oily Winship character. He'd rather proceed directly to investigating the hog lot.

Powell made a big to-do of knocking loudly at the door, to establish definitely no one was there. Then the Sheriff tacked the warrant to the door, making their search all very legal.

They walked toward one of the big hog confinement buildings, the one nearest them. The cerulean sky featured only a few fluffy clouds, product of the high humidity. It was a typical Iowa July day, except a little less torrid and sticky than usual.

They searched the American Heartland Hog Factory up and down, to and fro, thoroughly. But they found no hogs. There were a few piles of manure, producing a modest smell, but that was all.

"Like I said," droned Powell, "it is a puzzle."

The Sheriff nodded, repeating absently, "It's a puzzle."

They could not even find evidence of feed for hogs. Not a particle of anything of nutritional value could be found in the feeding areas. The troughs and all containers were bereft of the high-protein soy-and-corn-based meal that is the staple of a hog factory.

Powell threw up his hands in bewilderment. The Sheriff reflexively did the same. Just what in hell were they searching for?

Weeks went by. Summer became fall. Leaves turned red and yellow and fell. During this time, Winship could not be located and no activity could be discerned at the hog factory, except for the occasional goldfinch gliding to a brief stop on a fence post or a more frequent blue-and-tan barn swallow zigzagging frenetically low over the ground. No activity of any other sort, to be sure, at least that the Sheriff's deputies could detect. But at times there was still plenty of hog smell. And that was, of course, a big mystery.

During this time, the Sheriff's Department was busy with several drug cases. The Quinlan County Drug Task Force, comprised of city police officers, county deputies, and Iowa Division of Criminal Investigation personnel, was amassing evidence to prosecute methamphetamine producers and dealers. "Meth" is manufactured from a commonly used agricultural chemical, anhydrous ammonia, mixed with other chemicals, and "baked." The resultant substance is highly addictive and can easily cause a quick death. Iowa has had more than its share of such deaths.

A good deal of the meth used in Iowa was imported, usually from Mexico via California or Texas. But much of it was produced locally in a "lab," a word whose meanings include a bathroom in a motel room rented for a night or a kitchen in a farmhouse. Though Iowa had passed laws imposing a life sentence on dealers of meth to juveniles, the meth business was so profitable that greedy, uncaring individuals were still attracted to it. A secret lab in a house could produce huge profits, often using anhydrous ammonia stolen from nearby farms.

A meth bust in late November did not produce a lead related to the hog lot, but it provided a noteworthy correlation. The night the task force busted a lab at a farmhouse was also the night a tremendous smell emanated from the American Heartland Hog Factory. That, thought the Sheriff, was a curiosity worth investigating. Why would there be a huge smell from a hogless factory farm on the night of a big meth bust? The situation would not have warranted a raised eyebrow had it not been for his two bizarre visits to the hog lot.

But how to investigate? They had already been out there with a search warrant and found nothing. The Sheriff scratched his head. He needed to raid the hog lot **before** the next meth bust.

In a couple weeks, the task force was ready to strike. It informed the Sheriff and he swung into action four hours before the task force anticipated making a meth bust.

A deep orange and pink ribbon highlighted the western sky and the moon had begun to rise. The Sheriff's cruiser and three other Quinlan County squad cars sped toward the hog lot, wheeling up a plume of dust. They stopped suddenly, jumped from their cars, and ran toward the main buildings. Eight officers, weapons drawn, fanned out in order to cover all the buildings of the mega-facility. Their eyes grew quickly teary from a tremendous odor emanating from the hog lot. Each officer had to stop frequently in order to wipe blurry eyes with a handkerchief. They could not see well enough to continue without this self-treatment. For chrisesake, they really needed gas masks!

The officers examined one building after another. In the last building, they made an interesting find. In a large stainless steel tub, a brew of chemicals, including sulphate and ammoniate compounds, was undergoing a reaction. The vapors were being blown outside by a couple of huge, industrial-strength fans mounted on each side of the tub.

It smelled very bad. It wasn't exactly a hog smell when you got up close to it. But outside, it was inhaled as a very bad smell that most anyone would guess to be a hog problem, on account of there being a big hog lot in the vicinity.

The Iowa Division of Criminal Investigation and the Quinlan County Sheriff's Department launched an exhaustive investigation that absorbed over a thousand hours. They established that Steve Winship was, as the Sheriff put it, "impersonating a pig." In exchange for a cut in the meth labs' profits, he provided odiferous cover that enabled the labs within several miles of his hog lot to escape detection and produce huge batches of meth.

The DCI and the Sheriff could find no evidence implicating American Heartland Hog Factory officials above Winship. They did, however, conclude that Winship served as the fall guy for his superiors. There was simply no way they could not have known of his activities. But fall guy he was and the Sheriff gloated in referring to him as "the fallen pig."

Garbology, Iranian Style

Professor Rupert P. Hayes was looking forward to examining the garbage his Garbology class, Sociology 322-X, would bring in. The class came straight out of the sixties, an off-the-wall effort to apply Sociology in the year 2001. Dr. Hayes had earned his Ph.D. in the sixties at Berkeley. He concocted the course, a legacy of his years there. The idea is to look at garbage for evidence of social stratification, consumer trends, reading habits, and so on. What a person throws away is a kind of diary: it tells a lot about that person socially and personally.

Dr. Hayes was nearing age 64. He had balded to a gray fringed chaplet, and both his cholesterol and blood sugar registered substantially too high, testifying to the ineluctable passing of his allotted years. He had never married, though blessed with a good number of pathetic opportunities over the years. His college, colleagues and students, had become his family. In return for giving him a life and an income, he gave his college family brilliant courses like **Garbology In The Modern World.**

Dr. Hayes, in his office, at his desk piled high with books, articles, memos, and newspaper clippings, shrugged. He felt everyone should appreciate his brilliant contributions more, but, he knew he was clearly an intellectual ahead of his time. Great men were usually under-appreciated until after they died.

He swigged his decaf coffee from a mug from his alma mater that bore the Berkeley logo with the team name "Golden Bears" beneath it. A philosophical expression on his face, he uncrossed his legs that angled across his desk. He recrossed them and leaned back in his swivel chair, settling in for some serious thinking, about garbology, life, and whatever garbage slid down the chutes of his mind. A couple books and a pile of papers cascaded off his desk.

51

Prof Hayes' students would, in a few hours, go out into several neighborhoods of Quinlan, Iowa, from the ivied brick halls of Odin College, to collect garbage before the city did. The best time was about three a.m. Everyone who rolled their blaze-orange plastic garbage-can units to the curb would have done so by then. And the hour offered plenty of time before anyone stirred to enable his students to "dig garbage." Of course, he had notified the police as usual before his students went out. He didn't want any of his students mistaken for burglars and arrested, maybe even shot.

The affluent parents who paid tuition to Odin did not want their sons and daughters back in body bags. They didn't want them back at all, frankly. They wanted them to get degrees and leave home, to start lives, so they could return to the love stories that had produced their sons and daughters, at least those of them for whom a love story continued. But, for all, body bags would be unthinkable, an unsatisfactory, horrific chapter in their lives. They had paid tuition to a sanctuary like Odin, some consciously so, in order to fend off tragedy as well as to provide for a bright future for their kids.

The police had advised against the students doing archeological digs in local garbage. They had even consulted with the County Attorney. But the CA had said that once the garbage containers were curbside, the contents could be considered discarded, and were available for salvage efforts or garbological study prior to pick-up. He knew the ACLU would be pleased with his interpretation of the law, and so not wanting those "liberal hounds" on his case, he had issued an opinion to forestall any ACLU harassment when he had too much to do on an inadequate budget anyway.

Fourteen students were on the Garbology team. Thirteen women and one man. This gender imbalance owed to the facts that women comprised three-quarters of the Sociology majors and that women Soche students seemed, for some inexplicable reason, more attracted to Garbology. Year after year, it had been that way. He had not been able to figure out why. He kept thinking of Margaret Atwood's novel **Edible Woman**, where a woman's work in the kitchen never endured. It was eaten and the remains put into the garbage. Maybe it had something to do with that, with women subconsciously wanting to make durable, make a record of, women's traditional work. The professor scratched his head in its bald middle and looked up at the ceiling. Maybe that was it, an explanation imported from a Canadian author. Good as any. Nobody in Soche had bothered to do any serious research on the topic.

Linda Aikens and Joan Burken worked as a team. They were assigned to collect at four homes: 1011 Maize Heights, 392 Grove Street, 815 Gardella Avenue, and 16 Cooley Lane. They were to be finished at no later than 4:30 a.m.

Everything went smoothly till they got to 16 Cooley Lane. They had collected interesting "specimens" from the first three "garbology sites" (a play on "archeology sites," for the new field of Garbology considered Archeology to be one of its progenitors, along with Sociology and Anthropology). But 16 Cooley Lane at 4:06 a.m. proved a new experience.

Randomly selected, as per standard sociological research methodology, 16 Cooley Lane was home to Riley Ferguson, the CEO of Quinlan Corn and Soy. It loomed into view, as Linda and Joan walked from their car, that they had parked in a church parking lot. The home thrust three stories into the moonlight and the upflung light from the street lamps. It impressed the young women. It was a dream home. Maybe they one day would live in such a fabulous mansion, living good lives with a husband, children, and career they loved. The home would be a comfort, a major aid in living their lives, as well as a status symbol proclaiming their success over their peers.

Linda held a plastic garbage bag open while Joan deposited items they selected from #16 Cooley's garbage. They worked quietly, efficiently, making snap decisions under the street lights based on criteria Dr. Hayes had impressed upon them in lectures.

A discarded glove, a broken plate, a shirt, the remains of a microwaved dinner, several CDs and computer diskettes, and a pile of shredded paperwork from Quinlan Corn and Soy interested them. They began retrieving those items.

A stray dog that walked with a slight limp approached the two women. A friendly dog, she perceived Joan and Linda as the prospect for her next meal or even a home with a comfortable, pillow-lined wicker basket by a fireplace. She wagged her tail briskly, her yellow Labrador hair glowing under the streetlights. She stuck her muzzle into the plastic bag. Linda and Joan kept pulling it out, and she took to rubbing her head and body against them, in a kind of friendly getting-to-know-you, dog-bonds-with-people ritual.

Both Linda and Joan were disconcerted by the dog's antics. They became alarmed when the yellow Lab emitted a couple of ingratiating barks. "Let's get out of here," said Joan in a low voice. "This dog is going to get us into trouble."

Linda nodded emphatically, pulling out a wire tie, which she twisted around the mouth of the bag to seal it. "Enough Garbology for one night," she whispered.

The two young women beat a hasty, stealthy retreat, silent in their sneakers. They were about a block away from #16 Cooley when a light came on in the mansion. They were just turning a corner, and felt rather certain no one had seen them do anything suspicious. The person who turned on the light probably was responding to the yellow Lab's soft barks, if he was responding to anything at all. Someone may just have gotten up to raid the refrigerator.

They may have left #16 Cooley but the yellow Lab had not left them. Tongue hanging out and tail wagging, eyes bright, she had a certain bounce to her limping gait as she followed Joan and Linda to their car.

The yellow Lab pawed friendlily at the car door as Joan got into the driver's seat. He whined piteously after Linda had gotten in and put on her seat belt. Joan looked at Linda, "I can't leave this dog. She likes us. I like her. Let's take her back to the dorm."

Linda nodded and smiled.

Joan opened the door to the backseat, and the yellow dog jumped in, sat, and looked forward, as if to enjoy the ride. The dog was apparently a stray, but someone somewhere had treated her well. Or at least so Joan and Linda surmised. Perhaps the biggest prize to come out of the garbage hunt this morning would be a short-haired yellow dog with a friendly disposition!

Joan's creaky Cavalier emitted sounds symptomatic of advanced old age as it left the neighborhood. It threatened to wake someone, betraying their garbological venture. But, no one became alarmed. At least no lights came on. They had certainly done the right thing by parking the car in the church parking lot and walking to #16 Cooley. To have driven there would've awoken the entire Ferguson Family.

Joan, Linda, and the yellow Lab stopped for a coffee and Danish at the all-night truck stop at the edge of town. They fed a Danish to the dog who ate it ravenously. When Linda poured some coffee into a saucer, she lapped it up with gusto.

The waitress was amused. She liked the three of them, a perk to the dreary night shift. She said she didn't mind the dog as long as the dog was out of there before six a.m., when the next shift of waitresses and a cook arrived. That is about when the yellow Lab jumped gracefully onto a chair and sat as she ate her Danish and drank her coffee. It would've made an award-winning photo for a national newspaper, the two students and their newfound dog. There was something lugubrious, yet profoundly touching, about the three of them enjoying coffee and pastry at a table, surrounded by an empty salad bar, whacky-cat clocks with long tails tick-wagging behind the counter (all for sale), and the big semis visible in the wide restaurant windows, pulling in and out of the truck stop, their powerful headlights cutting big pieces out of the fading darkness.

It was a picture to soothe the heartache and disgust that the morning paper's headlines bring. It was a picture desperately needed as a countervailing good media force to the images and words about evil in the world that abound on front pages everywhere.

A soft yellow band was emerging on the eastern edge of Quinlan as Joan, Linda, and the dog drove to the residence hall at Odin College. The sun was making its ascent, promising a mild spring day for the college on a bluff overlooking the little town of Quinlan.

The yellow Lab seemed more than happy to be at Odin. She was excited. Jumping from the car, she ran in speedy circles about the vehicle and front lawn of Amundsen Hall. She gave off the air of a dog who had just happily ended her days as a stray. It was either that or the caffeine in the coffee she had recently consumed was taking effect.

Linda observed the dog and noted wryly, "She's real energetic. Enroll her in Dr. Hayes' class. She could really be good at Garbology, get a lot done."

Joan gave a short laugh. "We'll keep her in our room in Amundsen until we figure out what to do."

Though the morning paper may have required a human-interest photo of two women and a dog, the evening paper required a photo of salvation, one of redeeming compassion. The evening headline proved a tectonic-plate shock to Linda and Joan. The Ferguson Family at #16 Cooley had been murdered. The bodies of the father, Quinlan Corn and Soy CEO Riley Ferguson and his wife Dorothy were found in their second-story bedroom. The bodies of the two daughters, Tricia and Alicia, were found in their third-story bedroom. There was no disarray that one would expect had there been a struggle. Apparently, the four had been killed without an opportunity to resist their fates.

Joan and Linda did not know what to do at first. The **Quinlan Quotient** quoted the police as saying the murders took place, judging from an examination of the bodies, in the wee hours of the morning. That meant they were doing Garbology 322-X at exactly the wrong time. Yet. they could contribute nothing by reporting their experience. At least not yet. And certainly, right now, they were far too upset to report anything.

They decided to say nothing, to try and calm down, and go about their assignment of sorting and analyzing the garbage they had collected. They also had to care for their new companion whom they called simply "yellow Lab," as a kind of generic way of classifying a creature that had entered their lives basically uninvited.

"It shakes me up to think that we were there just about the time the Fergusons were murdered," intoned Linda.

"Maybe we should tell Dr. Hayes," said Joan. "He may not recognize that #16 Cooley is the Ferguson home right away."

Linda shrugged. "Let's sort this stuff first. Maybe we can decide whether to go to him while we're doing this."

They sat across from each other, each sitting at the edge of her own bed, as they arrayed the contents of the Ferguson bag out before them on a newspaper, whose several sections they had spread out to cover the floor space between them. Yellow Lab sat alertly, thinking the entire activity was designed for her amusement.

Joan forced a laugh. "Yellow Lab thinks we have devised a game just for her."

Linda leaned toward the dog. "Just so you don't stick your nose into this stuff again, you can think whatever you want." Yellow Lab's ears twitched and he gave off a low, almost human-sounding guttural sound. "She knows we're talking about her."

Joan smiled wanly. "She's an intelligent poochie. She has to be. She's now part of our Garbology class."

Both the young women laughed nervously, an unaccustomed furriness in their throats.

The contents of the Ferguson bag began to emerge. Linda listed them on a notepad as Joan extracted them. Discarded glove, but no blood O. J. Simpson style. Broken plate, but no clue there.

Linda blurted, "Y'know, I'm acting like a detective. Look what I've written."

Joan peered at the notebook. "This is no longer a Garbology exercise, is it? It's an investigation."

Linda nodded somberly. The inventory continued.

What drew their attention was the shredded paper from Quinlan Corn and Soy. Why had it been shredded? Was there any way to reconstruct it? Maybe computer technology would give them a way. They would have to consult Dr. Hayes. If he didn't know, he had the college's Computer Information Systems Department to consult.

Joan patted the yellow Lab on the head. "We need to leave you while we see Dr. Hayes. But we're leaving you a bowl of water. Enjoy."

Joan and Linda left the room, but the dog howled so piteously that Linda had to return and dog-sit. Yellow Lab seemed content with that arrangement. As Joan went out of Amundsen Hall and walked toward Nansen Hall, she heard no more howling.

The campus had thrown off its winter pallor. The trees, shrubs, and flower beds presented a vibrancy of brightness and delicacy of pastel for the eyes to feast on. The lilacs, daffodils, and crocuses had just begun their renewal in the varying season. The stark silhouettes along St. Olaf Drive had leafed out with a compelling life that refreshed the senses and lifted the spirit, proving that within them resided the essence of everything that is maple and elm and basswood. Dr. Hayes had once referred in class to this leafing process as an "excellent metaphor for Odin College's educational process."

Dr. Hayes was expecting her. She had told him by phone from the dorm room about their Garbology work at the Ferguson mansion. "Where is Linda?" he asked as Joan came through the doorway.

"She had to stay with the yellow Lab."

Prof Hayes' eyes registered question marks.

"A stray dog we took in for a while. Walks with a limp. Needs some nursing."

Prof Hayes clasped his hands over his chest, leaning back in his swivel chair. As usual, his scruffy, gray fringe was beset by a rebellion of hair, taking off in every whichway disarray. "So you think you may have some possible clue in the shredded paper?...Well, to tell the truth, I don't think there is any high-tech way to put it together." He paused. "But there is a low-tech way."

Joan's eyes widened in puzzlement.

"You weren't yet born when the Iranians took over our embassy in 1979. When they did that, the student radicals found lots of shredded secret papers. Our CIA and State Department assumed that shredding rendered them unusable. But that assumption didn't prove out."

"How so?"

"Well, the Iranians got teams together to piece together the tiny strips until they made sense. It took a lot of time to do the many top-secret files, but they finally did it, through trial and error, many thousands of hours. Then they translated everything into their main language, Farsi."

"But we don't have thousands of hours!" exclaimed Joan.

"Yes," replied Prof Hayes. "But we have only a small amount of shredded material—about five pounds you said over the phone—compared to the thousands of pounds the Iranians had to process. Our Garbology class of fourteen should be able to piece it together in a few days, working a little a day. Since this could conceivably uncover a clue to the murders, I'll devote the class's time to it."

Joan smiled again. Before she left, she shook the Prof's hand, something she had never done before.

Over the next few days, the Garbology class painstakingly reconstructed the shredded paper. A lot of nerves frayed and fingers wore down beyond endurance. But through the camaraderie and collective effort that perhaps only a class of group-oriented Sociology majors could muster so magnificently, a total reconstruction was achieved. Some items pieced together proved to be innocuous faxes or e-mails. But one seemed to have potential as a lead to finding the murderer or murderers of the Fergusons.

Linda felt so emotionally and physically spent that she threatened to petition the college for an extra three hours of credit, in Criminology. Prof Hayes, realizing it would be impolitic to reject her idea out of hand, said that it might be a good idea, provided the Academic Dean approved her petition. He even encouraged her to fill out a petition for the extra credit, and told her that the appropriate form was available in the Registrar's Office.

He may have never had children of his own but he prided himself in being sensitive to the feelings of his students. That sort of **simpatico** regard for them had made him quite popular over the years, more so than many of his colleagues a generation younger. This was a source of immense pride for him. He may look like a man past his prime, but he could relate to young people!

The Garbology class reassembled one fax that intrigued them. It was from one John Dillman of Des Moines who had waxed irate that his stores had not been regularly supplied with the sugar that Quinlan Corn and Soy produced from corn. It was an odd business message, fraught with anger, and it provoked their interest. Probably it was nothing. But Dillman's ire was the only forceful emotion to speak from the shredded paper.

Prof Hayes turned over the Dillman fax to the Quinlan P.D., along with the entire bag of Ferguson items. Chief Delbert Venzke, a burly monolith of a man about ten years Hayes' junior, thanked him for his assistance. "Maybe this Dillman fax will yield something," he said, though on the face of it, he couldn't see how. He shrugged inwardly. But he'd take any assistance, albeit unpromising on the surface, even if from a balding, eccentric college professor who seemed to have dottered to the edge of senility.

Prof Hayes smiled broadly. "It is my privilege to assist the Quinlan P.D.," he said effusively.

What a putz, thought Chief Venzke. These guys really do live in an ivory tower!

Prof Hayes left the police station, proud of the new discipline of Garbology's contribution to police investigation. His class, all fourteen of them, ought to be very proud. Perhaps he ought to shred the usual grade curve and award them all an A for service beyond the course requirements! He walked to his car, absorbed in thought, scratching the center of his baldness, and feeling very macho.

Chief Venzke contacted the Iowa Division of Criminal Investigation. The DCI checked Dillman for a record and paid him a visit. After a great deal of leg work, phone calls, and checking all avenues, the DCI concluded that Dillman was simply the owner of three family stores, unconnected to a big grocery chain, that was being stiffed a bit on its orders of sugar. He was assuredly no suspect.

It has been almost two years since the murders of the Fergusons. Today, the case has been relegated to a back burner. The Quinlan P.D. and DCI pursue an occasional fruitless lead, but that is all. For all their massive efforts in the days and weeks immediately after the murders, they could find no one who could qualify as a suspect armed with a .22 caliber pistol to which a silencer had probably been attached.

Only the yellow Lab knows, and she, of course, is not talking, at least not in a comprehensible way. Joan, who has graduated with her B.A. in Sociology from Odin College and now works for the Department of Human Services in Quinlan, owns the yellow Lab. Sometimes when the dog is haunched on the passenger-side seat of the Cavalier as Joan runs errands around town, she sees or smells the murderer. She barks louder than usual, trying to tell Joan.

The yellow Lab might as well be speaking Farsi.

Stealthily, Like A Cat

Professor David Ward was furious. For the third consecutive year, he had been denied a salary increase. "Politics!" he shrilled. "Just because I'm trying to organize a union, they're really sticking it to me!" He paused, looking hard at his wife Noreen over the breakfast table. Lowering his voice to a near-growl, he added, "But I'll get even."

"What do you mean?" Noreen asked uneasily. "You're not the kind to seek revenge."

"Revenge?" cried Dr. Ward. "This is not revenge! This is self-defense. I'm angry because I'm getting screwed, because they're walking all over me!"

On second thought, Noreen felt she had had enough, too, enough of turning the other cheek. She could feel her fighting blood rising. They had wanted a new car to replace their twelve-year-old Oldsmobile. That idea had died with the first lost salary increase. They had wanted to take a trip to Mazatlan, but denied salary increment number two had wasted that notion. After the third freeze of Dave's salary, they had cashed in an IRA in order to replace their leaky roof and install siding on the house. She did not even want to begin to contemplate the lost opportunities that might accompany another denied salary increase. The more she dwelt on the issue, the angrier she became.

No Ph.D. with ten years of university study under his belt and eighteen years of teaching experience should be subjected to such shabby treatment. She had worked and scrimped and saved, the faithful wife, to help upgrade their life. And now this: a fear of financial starvation. Would there be missed salary increment number four?

Noreen put a hand to her mouth. What would number four do to them? Would number four bring them both destructive neuroses for which they could afford no psychotherapy? She dropped her hand and clasped it tightly over the edge of the

63

table. She knew they must fight back. But how? "What can we do, Dave?" she asked, her voice laden with emotion.

President Hakeem Obunsula pondered angrily the scurrilous accusations Professor Ward had hurled at him in the gadfly scandal sheet, **The Academic Scum Shoveler.**

He swiveled in his executive, leather-upholstered chair, leaned forward and pulled out a file containing the most recent **Scum Shovelers.** Fanning out the contents on his desk, he didn't know which one to read first. Each seemed equally sleazy and libelous, well deserving of his ire. Each provoked his desire to get even with Professor Ward. All were his "favorites." Yet, thumbing through the collection, he found one that had especially twerked him off. It was headed "President Obunsula's Speech Stinks." It featured a cutting analysis of his "State of the College" address, listing sixteen syntactical clangers, twelve word misuses, three mispronunciations, and two verb tense mistakes. Funny, very funny! A professor ought to show some deference to his boss.

He knew why Dr. Ward had so little respect. He had never done any military service. Inquiry by the Quinlan Community College police had revealed that Ward had been granted conscientious objector status during the Vietnam War. So much bullshit. That damn Ward had become a C.O. at the very time he had been heroically fighting Ibo and Yoruba insurgents back home in Nigeria where he had been seriously wounded for his efforts.

Granted, his injury had come during coitus with an attractive captured guerrilla terrorist. He had fallen off. Grasping frantically for anchorage as he took leave of the bed, he had latched onto the neck of a lamp, going down with it. It had splintered into him and he had been hospitalized.

The army doctors had operated on him for "glass shrapnel" as they laughingly put it, out of earshot. But what was the shame in it? The vast majority of the Nigerian Army were frequenting prostitutes to fill the needs of bodies that might not see the next sunrise. His only misdeed had been that the female guerrilla terrorist had taken advantage of his fall and escaped.

Dr. Obunsula muttered, "I'll show that pacifist. Damn him." He gathered the **Scum Shovelers** and threw them violently across his office. As they settled, he shouted, "You'll never get another salary increase here! You belong over at Odin College where they like this kind of stuff!"

Professor Ward finished the most caustic piece he had ever written for **The Academic Scum Shoveler.** Yet he did not feel the usual elation after scoring a muckraking coup over the administration. This time, he felt only depressed. How many times had he done this only to suffer for it?

Perhaps this sort of academic response to bureaucratic oppression was inadequate. He puckered his brow in contemplation, trying to think of something he could do. After a lengthy silence, his eyes lit up. He had a great idea.

He crumpled his ill-advised piece of muckraking journalism and tossed it toward the waste basket. Unfortunately, he missed and scored a perfect shot into his recently poured cup of decaf coffee.

He grimaced. What next?

Professor Ward applied the finishing touches to his disguise as Noreen set his jet-black wig onto his balding dome. As the black thing settled snugly onto its spot of skin, he examined himself in the mirror. He could hardly believe it was the same Professor Ward. The modish hairpiece, the mascara on the eyebrows, the tinted glasses, and trendy new clothes made him look very different. President Obunsula would never recognize him until it was too late. The evil administrator would be his prisoner before he knew what hit him.

President Obunsula stood at a window overlooking a park. It was, he thought, proving to be a great party. Everyone who was anyone in the college town had been invited and most everyone invited was putting in at least a brief appearance. A good number were staying an hour or more, enjoying the canapés, drinks, and convivial bonhomie. His seventh annual spring semester party looked like a smashing success.

President Obunsula chuckled inwardly. He knew how to hold onto power. To be sure, he had to do the basic job as president, but mostly his role consisted of PR and making friends with the right people so that the local powerbrokers and the governing board did not ease him out. That was his Machiavellian view.

Obunsula saw an unfamiliar, glasses-wearing, black-haired man enter. It might be, he guessed, someone new to the community, a businessman perhaps, that his wife had put on the invitation list. He would have to introduce himself at the earliest opportunity.

That fellow who had just arrived, to be counted among those who wielded power in the city, was indeed weird-looking. Apparently not all the weird people in town were faculty. He could recognize all those, front, back, and profile, owing to his frequent referrals to the computerized faculty registry, compiled by his campus police. The new arrival was not faculty. He was a mystery. Who could he be?

Perhaps the new arrival had inherited wealth and now exerted tremendous anonymous influence. If you enjoyed that kind of bequested situation, you could afford to be eccentric.

Dr. Ward mixed with the guests, avoiding speaking beyond one or two words. He knew it would be difficult to disguise his voice in longer utterances. Someone could easily recognize him.

He quietly ladled a cup of punch and studiously became immensely absorbed in the beverage, a convenient way to isolate himself. He had to be single-minded in the pursuit of his quarry, for his mission was clear.

His sole aim was to capture President Obunsula. He would bide his time until he could pounce. Anticipating the vengeance that would soon be his, he savored the punch. He might be the pariah par excellence of the Quinlan Community College faculty, but he would create his own dignity through action, authenticating himself and shaping the meaning of his life in true existentialist fashion. He would take Frantz Fanon and Herbert Marcuse's advice and let his authentic self emerge from his own unique action.

The punch wasn't half-bad, considering it was Obunsula's. Dr. Ward returned to the punch bowl and refilled. He had begun to feel really good and wished he could freely talk with the guests. But he had to keep his mission uppermost in mind. The hundred-odd people in the house were the arch-consorts of his arch-enemy and no compromise, no matter how much internal warmth the punch conferred, was possible.

This was war, or at least the moral equivalent of it. He only wished he could kidnap and ransom all the guests, along with that odious, unctuous saw-off who impersonated a college president. "Chief Executive Officer" he liked to call himself, as if he were a captain of industry condescending to preside over an aggregation of academics who badly need an "Officer" to lead them military-style.

Professor Ward was proud that Obunsula had run into "stress management" problems with those such as himself who sought only the truth as the existential foundation of their lives. Those problems imposed only fair-to-middling stress compared to the serious stress he was about to inflict!

The professor shifted his hairpiece, that he imagined had slid askew. Then he enjoyed a helping of finger food—petits fours and dainty little sandwiches. He wiped the back of his hand across his forehead. He felt hot. The cumulative effect of the punch on his complex personality structure, housed in the unusually intricate convolutions of his brain, assailed him with misgivings about kidnapping Obunsula.

He began to feel very nervous about the .25-caliber pistol hidden under his jacket. He had never fired a gun before. What if he had to use it? That was out of the question. He was not capable of actually firing the weapon. Kidnapping wouldn't do. Too much chance of violence. How could he ever explain to his Conflict Resolution and Peacemaking class that he had accidentally killed the president of the college?

Dr. Ward experienced a sudden surge, an epiphany. He had a better idea. He would kidnap and ransom the Obunsulas' white-striped orange cat, which had appeared several times at the kitchen doorway.

Stealthily, like a cat, he made his way to the kitchen, where he befriended the cat by feeding it leftovers from the refrigerator. What luck! He was alone with the cat. After providing a few tasty morsels, he enticed the purring tabby to follow him out the back door. He dangled a delectable morsel before her all the way to his car. There he gave the animal the tidbit and locked her in. She sat on the front seat, enjoying her food, purring contentedly.

He had done it! He had kidnapped Obunsula by proxy, through his cat. It had not been necessary to capture the president. Only a fool would do that. He had seized the president's cat, and that ought to bring in the highest possible ransom, enough to recoup the three lost salary increases. Obunsula's wife would never let her cat die, whatever the price.

As he drove away, Professor Ward tried to recall Obunsula's wife's name and whether he had ever met her.

Leo's Memories

Leo Campbell debated with himself as he drove I-80. Should he take the next exit and visit his old hometown? He hadn't been there in over thirty years. That was on the plus side of the ledger in the debate. Yet, on the negative side, he had to consider that he no longer knew anyone in Quinlan, Iowa. The thought of visiting his home town as a stranger in his old age made him feel uneasy. But Quinlan still offered some of the old familiar sights of his youth. And so, at the very last second, he swerved hard off the interstate. He was going home. After all, it was the only hometown he had.

It was a gorgeous July day. Goldenrod, Queen Anne's lace, brown-eyed susans, and milkweed bearing pastel-pink flowers nodded in gentle breezes along fencerows guarding maturing fields of corn. Leo thought the rural landscape of his youth resplendently beautiful. He gasped audibly with pleasure at the view. How life in urban New Jersey had removed him from the rural joys!

He could feel a sense of connection return and could see himself in his mind's eye. Leo, the young, small-town kid climbing an apple tree in neighbor John Harrison's yard. There, straddling a branch, his back against the trunk, he had stuffed himself with russet apples till the prospect of climbing down seemed vastly uncomfortable. So, he waited and gazed at the sky through the leaves at the cottony clouds shape-shifting high in the pale-blue sky, morphing into many shapes as they rapidly tumbled. He recalled how he liked to imagine different shapes as various animals and even as his relatives. Sometimes he would bring the two morph categories together, and suddenly a pig with Uncle Ed's face would emerge from the billowy white. Or, he would discern a cow that wore Aunt Mary's face. He had a lot of fun with clouds that way, and he laughed a lot over his creations.

69

Sitting in his screened-in back porch, smoking a pipe, languidly rocking in his chair, John Harrison failed to see Leo until the purple twilight of evening had silhouetted the boy. Surprised, he jumped up. "Have you had enough apples to eat?" he called up to the boy.

Leo looked down sheepishly into the shadows of the porch. "Please don't tell my mother," he requested. "I'll mow your lawn if you don't tell. I'll do anything if you don't tell."

"I won't tell," returned Harrison, whose main concern was that Leo might fall from his tree. He appeared from the porch and looked directly at Leo. "Do me a favor, will you? Wait till I get a ladder so you can get down safely. You're way up there in my tree. I don't want you to get hurt."

Harrison hustled into his shed and brought out a weathered ladder, the kind designed for picking fruit, with a third leg that swings out in order to prop it in place. He positioned the ladder so that Leo could easily step onto an upper rung and descend.

It proved a delicate operation getting down. Leo had climbed higher than was safe. Harrison exhaled in relief as Leo stepped off the bottom rung onto the ground. "You don't have to mow my lawn, or do anything. I'm just glad you're safe." He riveted a disapproving glare on the boy. "I only ask that next time you want apples, come ask for permission. I'll let you have apples, but I want to be around to be sure you don't get hurt."

Harrison had died long ago, but that early lesson in responsibility had endured as real and vibrant as if it had happened yesterday. He had been spared him his mother's wrath and his father's strap. Leo had always been grateful for that. He had never again acted so foolishly.

Leo recalled vividly, over almost seven decades, how he had first reacted to Harrison by requesting that his Mom not be told. Mom was always the first contact for him, and he had often wondered why. After he had left home to attend college, when he phoned home, he always asked for his Mom first, even if Dad answered. After a few sparse words at most, Mom would take the phone and conduct the conversation, maybe letting Dad have the last few words, if he hadn't in the meantime gone outside to do some errand like watering the garden or shoveling snow. It seemed throughout his youth that his Dad hovered in the background in domestic scenes as his Mom took the responsibility for communication.

Leo had long ago concluded that this was a cultural pattern. His college roommate experienced a similar phone-home routine. Both of them felt uneasy talking with their fathers, though they had learned to be comfortable in their presence.

Leo reflected whether the past sixty years had advanced him anywhere except closer to the grave. His image of the nimble ten-year-old who enjoyed fresh russet apples, crisply, with teeth he no longer had, prompted feelings of bittersweet nostalgia. Youthfulness should perhaps be something you should advance toward over the years rather than retreat from, he conjectured acidly. That might make more sense of a life.

He sighed and surveyed the eternal waves of corn that suddenly made him feel insignificant. He drove a new Lincoln Town Car by the expanses of corn. Yet, the car he had bought to master the road and insulate himself from insecurity no longer served that purpose. For the first time he could recall, he felt a loss of importance in the scheme of things. Maybe **futile** was a better word. Was it the sea of corn? Or his advanced old age? His mind offered up a mix of emotions that he could not fully fathom.

The county road into Quinlan impressed him as the same old blacktop that his friend Kenny Williams had died on during their junior year. Kenny had careened down the road alone, hell-bent on testing the limits that held him earthbound. And for his recklessness, he had lost his life.

It seemed unreal to be driving the county blacktop sixty-one years after Kenny had died. They had often driven down this road together in the old Ford they had fixed up. They had shared great times and had been the best of friends.

Kenny's mother was inconsolable the night she was told that her son had crashed the Ford into a huge cottonwood tree beside the road. After the funeral, where she broke down completely, she would not leave her home for several weeks, even to go shopping.

Kenny's father presented a stoic exterior as he mourned the loss of his only son. He pushed himself through the weeks ahead, by a force of will, numb to all about him. Only dogged routine, and steely determination, made him seem like the same man. He had held himself together, but under the appearance lay a profoundly changed man.

Leo felt a bit peeved at himself and a lot guilty that he could not remember the names of Kenny's parents. He consoled himself with the fact that they had left Quinlan about a year after the accident. That is why he could not remember, he assured himself.

The cottonwood that claimed Kenny's life stood not far from the family home, where his mother had suffered horrid nightmares. Spreading its massive branches, the "evil tree". had snatched her son from her, off the blacktop. The wisps of cotton that floated vernally from the tree represented, not regeneration to her, but death. She dreamed that the transparent bits of fluff were shreds of Kenny's soul that the devil in that tree was sending to hell.

The sight of the tree, the inevitable driving past it, had proven too painful to endure. Kenny's parents moved away, to somewhere out West. Leo vaguely recalled hearing while he was still in college that they had ended up near Spokane, Washington. But that, of course, was long ago. They had long since died.

Just before they moved, the big tree caught on fire. The fire department extinguished the blaze in a few minutes, but the tree was mortally wounded. It would live a couple more years, yet, during that time, it produced only a small portion of the foliage it had so gloriously offered in the past and little of the wispy cotton that broadcast its seed. Its decline measured the revenge that everyone knew Kenny's father had taken on it with gasoline and match.

Leo wondered what would have happened had he been with Kenny that fateful evening. Maybe the accident would never have happened. He would have insisted that Kenny slow down. The tree would have been just another tree, like thousands of others around Quinlan. It would have had a natural history but it would not become the last split-second of a personal history. And the tree would never have been immolated in a desperate **auto-da-fé**, ignited by a distraught father destroying an heretical tree.

As he drove by the spot where the tree once stood, Leo wished he could return to age sixteen and make events come out differently. So far, on his drive into Quinlan, he realized with an inward start, he had wanted to return to two of his former existences: the apple-eating ten-year-old and the lanky sixteen-year-old. He wanted the innocent, carefree life of the young boy with his simple joys of delicious apples. But even more, he wanted to reoccupy his age-sixteen body so that he could convert a tragedy into a near-miss. The old Ford would just miss the cottonwood and come to an abrupt, jolting, safe stop.

Tears flowed freely as Leo thought about what might have been, what ought to have been. Kenny should have lived a long life, as he had done. But the old Ford, the blacktop, and the cottonwood had together violently extracted the "ought" from the future, killing Kenny amid the wreckage of his own impulsivity.

Leo drove down the main street of Quinlan. The downtown was still recognizable, although it had lost a good deal of its vitality. Gorman's Drugstore was boarded up. So were Zeller's Department Store and a few others.

The downtown had gone downhill, as one store after another had become vacant. A lot of shopping was now done in the mall outside town. Quinlan itself was increasingly being passed by.

As the blue sky deepened into evening, Leo thought that only old men with their memories traveled to the downtown anymore. Their memories were more substantial than the decaying buildings and boarded-up storefronts, and those memories gave them a place to visit in the downtown.

Leo drove back toward I-80, traveling into the time of day when quietness invades the Iowa landscape and takes up residence in all the things one sees. Every stalk of corn, every tree, every cloud, every farmhouse is suddenly still. Each can be seen with preternatural clarity. In a fleeting moment, the destiny of each thing is revealed and crystallized in memory.

Coffins

The Vietnam War was still raging and Jim was still very angry. He had been angry for years. He was thinking angry thoughts as he took the freeway exit ramp, arriving in Oakland to visit his brother, Larry, at his job as a dispatcher for the Western Pacific Railroad. He wanted to see those "coffins." The very thought of them made him angrier.

The "coffins," as Larry referred to them, were the aluminum cadaver transport containers, ACTCs in military parlance—they snapped shut and locked—that the military used to transport dead soldiers from Vietnam to Oakland, California. From there, they were sent to destinations around the country, back to their grieving families.

Dozens of bodies were arriving weekly that July. The Western Pacific Railroad was doing a terrific business in an "important commodity, dead farm kids from the Midwest," thought Jim acidly. Or, at least, it seemed almost all the bodies were going there, especially to Iowa and South Dakota.

Larry had said he couldn't believe how many kids from Iowa and South Dakota had gone to Vietnam and returned dead. From his viewpoint as a dispatcher, arranging final trips home, Vietnam looked like a holocaust for those two states. "Last week was especially bad for a town named Quinlan, Iowa," he had commented by phone last night. "Three coffins!" Neither of them had ever heard of Quinlan before, but they felt they owed it to the mourning families somehow, to at least look it up on the map.

Jim pulled into the parking lot at the Oakland railroad depot, a long, mission-style, pastel-yellow, stucco building. The WP had built all its depots in this style. Although they varied according to the size of the town or city, the same basic model was evident. He felt comfortable parking beside such a familiar-looking building, even though it stood in a poor, crowded part of downtown.

He had driven from Oroville, a Sacramento Valley town, relentlessly hot, sizzling to 100 degrees and above. Oakland, on the San Francisco Bay, offered cool air that provided welcome relief. The cooler air also offered a decided military advantage: "The better to preserve dead bodies!" Jim muttered cynically to himself.

After negotiating the heavy Bay Area traffic, Jim felt tense as he unfolded his tall frame from the car. Four hours of travel from uncongested, rural California to a teeming city had made him stiff. Once his feet stood firmly on asphalt, he stretched his limbs in several directions and touched his toes in order to limber up.

Most the people Jim saw in the street were black passersby going to and from stores, jobs, and various errands. He wondered where the black bodies from the Oakland ghetto went when they returned to California. The WP did not handle those, yet there were a large number of them to account for. Who handled those? If you tallied for the entire State of California, blacks were an unfair share of the war dead. Someone besides the WP was doing a land-office business.

Two young boys were playing marbles directly beside the depot. One was white, the other black. Both smiled at Jim as he passed. He smiled back.

As Jim entered the depot, he could see that Larry was busy with a "consist," putting together a train to run into Nevada. Larry smiled at him to acknowledge his arrival, but he could not stop to talk. He had to continue his last-minute pressured work, lots of paperwork and phone calls, to finalize arrangements to send the dead soldiers home. Each corpse would follow its own separate route once the train reached the Midwest. The paperwork for each young body needed to be correct.

Jim took a seat in the waiting room, joining a few people who were waiting for the passenger train, the **Zephyr**. He would not be joining them, but he envied them, for he always enjoyed traveling on the silver train comprised of "dome cars" with splendid views, ranging from the rice paddies near Sacramento, and the oak groves near Oakland, to the precipitous canyons of the Feather River. As he settled onto a high-backed pine bench, he tried to make himself comfortable as he waited for his brother. He sat back and studied the cigarette smoke curling toward the ceiling where it was whisked over the room by a fan.

A man seated directly across from him was reading the **Oakland Tribune.** The front page proclaimed a high Vietcong body count for the week just ended. Jim felt uneasy at the sight of the headline over a story covering recent battles in the Pleiku region. He felt irritated at the man for inadvertently inclining the paper toward him so he could not avoid reading the headlines.

Jim believed the papers had been complicit in playing up VC casualties and downplaying the Americans' losses. The **Tribune** had proved no exception.

He had a friend in France who had noted in recent letters how very different the war looked in the French media. He needed to send that friend, whom he had met at the University of California, some clippings from the American press. At long last, things had gotten so bad that public opinion had begun to turn heavily against the war. The papers would soon have to curb their boosterism of war and death.

Jim unfolded his news magazine over his knee. He popped a stick of gum into his mouth. He decided to read the book and movie reviews to avoid the inevitable pages on Vietnam and to keep from looking at the man's paper across from him. As he read, he looked up occasionally to enjoy the scene about him that included a young woman and her baby, and a family—a mom, dad, and three kids—all the while averting his eyes from the **Oakland Tribune** before him.

The war had upset him for years. Perhaps he was too sensitive, some of his relatives argued. He should take the war in stride, they said, live each day to the full. But he believed they were altogether too insensitive about the war. He felt the pain of the victims of the war, American and Vietnamese, in an almost personal way. Yes, his alleged "hypersensitivity" had dampened the quality of his days during the war, making him too angry for his own good, but that was something he was very proud of. No one should be extraordinarily happy in a society that is filling thousands of coffins with young soldiers.

Like a huge epidemic that spared some, the draft had passed him by. The military had given him a physical at the Oakland Induction Center three times, each time classifying him 1-Y. That classification meant that he had minor physical problems that made him unfit for service—congenitally flat feet and fifty pounds of excess weight—but that he could be conscripted if necessary, if the war grew larger. He jested inwardly that they examined him the second and third times to see if he had been foolish enough to go on a diet as well as somehow miraculously grow insteps for his flat feet!

As the slanting afternoon sun highlighted motes of dust and curls of cigarette smoke in the upper air of the waiting room, making them appear to dance lazily, he forgot the discomforting **Tribune** headlines and began to enjoy himself, a rare occasion in recent years. Long had he felt constrained, stressed, like the nation, ever since the war had begun. Perhaps the next stage in his life would be guilt. Many were still dying.

A war can wreak havoc on a psyche in insidious ways. Without the war, his life, like millions of others, would be able to unfold in more natural, harmonious, fluid ways rather than be delimited by concerns over killing and dying, endings rather than beginnings.

As Jim finished the book reviews and began the section on sports, he looked up, startled to find the woman with the baby standing over him. "Will you hold my baby for a minute?" she asked.

Without asking why, Jim set aside his magazine and gathered the baby into his arms. The little body felt strange, as though it didn't belong in his arms. How could a woman just up and do that? She didn't know him. Yet she had dumped her baby into his arms, literally.

The baby made some movements with its mouth, like maybe it wanted to eat or drink. Jim didn't know what to do, so he puckered his mouth and made some squeegee sounds.

The baby began to cry. Heads turned his way, and Jim was sure he was blushing. He wished that the mother would return immediately. He could only endure so much.

After about four minutes—it seemed much longer as he followed the minute hand on the wall clock—he was relieved to see her again. "Thank you," she said evenly as she retrieved her crying baby.

In about ten minutes, a train departed the Oakland depot. One car contained the neatly stacked aluminum coffins of young Vietnam soldiers, dead before their time.

The baby did not stop crying until the train had disappeared from view. It was just coincidence he knew, but Jim liked to think that the baby had cried for the dead soldiers. Someone should cry, he thought. The train was not just another train.

Jim returned to his **Newsweek**, resolving to find Quinlan, Iowa, on the map as his next major priority.

G. Louis Heath, Ph. D.

The Lynching Of The Mysterious Wyoming Cowboy

(In memory of Matthew Shepard, lynched outside Laramie, October, 1998)

He rode into town wearing a white Stetson hat, a black duster, leather chaps, and dusty boots of a nondescript color. Furtive glances were cast in his direction as he hitched Old Paint in front of the saloon. The townsfolk were confused because they couldn't stereotype the guy as a good guy wearing white or a bad guy wearing black. He had confused them by wearing both black and white! And his horse was a multicolored brindled thing that defied description, amounting to a kind of camouflage, offering them no clue whatsoever.

It was a hot day and the wind kicked up swirls of fine pale brown dust. Everyone who could was chilling out in the shade or slaking parched throats with high-proof whiskey. The horses hitched at the saloon were miserably hot under the beating sun, suffering a tortured, prolonged heat exhaustion. They resented their owners inside, drinking whiskey, sheltered from the brain-and-skin-frying sun.

They got to neighing and snorting among themselves, communicating in their argot of Wyoming-horse-gab, low and guttural, which from a distance sounded a lot like Norwegian or Low German. They decided, democratically, on a six-to-two vote, that they were going to—if they could manage to get unhitched—kick some Wyoming cowboy ass, especially that of the Mysterious Wyoming Cowboy.

The townspeople understood. Stealthily, they unhitched the miserable horses, all eight of them, including the two who had voted against hooving the asses of the horse-abusing Wyoming cowboys into oblivion, onto the dusty high-plains horizon. The townspeople could groove on that because they knew that the inscrutable cowboy just arrived would be among those who got his comeuppance. If the horses kicked his ass out of town, any danger he might pose to them would be removed.

Certainly, enabling the horses to horse up on the cowboy was easier than stereotyping him. Why didn't he fit into some kind of mold so they would know how to deal with him? Why, his very individualism was a threat to the orderly flow of life in their little one-saloon town!

The sun throbbed, an intense golden disc hanging high over the high chaparral, as the Mysterious Wyoming Cowboy flung open squeakily the twin, slatted, batwing doors of the saloon. He was well practiced at holding his whiskey, but still he walked a little unsteadily, his senses a bit diminished.

He was vulnerable.

Before he could draw his gun, the horses were upon him. Their hooves flew ferociously as they let fly their hatred for the Mysterious Wyoming Cowboy and all cowboys in general. Soon, they had hooved his ass into a sorry state.

The townspeople helped the horses slip a noose over his neck. As he felt the noose tighten, the Mysterious Wyoming Cowboy wished desperately that he had worn a completely white outfit. Then the people would have never projected their amorphous hostilities onto him. They would have bought him a drink instead of unhitching the horses.

And there would have been no lynching of the Mysterious Wyoming Cowboy.

G. Louis Heath, Ph. D.

Lady Luck And The Mud Cat

Everyone in town called it "the boat." It, the **Mud Cat,** a casino sternwheeler, spent most its time moored at a dock near downtown Quinlan, on the Mississippi River. A couple hours each day, it cruised upriver a few miles to lock and dam number 17, and back. In the summer, entertainment was provided—a singer who accompanied herself on guitar or banjo, or a small oom-pah-pah or Country-Western band. Tourists made Quinlan their destination in order to ride the boat, listen to the music, and, of course, to gamble.

The boat did a thriving business, drawing locals and out-of-towners in droves. The Iowa government that authorized the boat cynically called it "entertainment." This was the same government that busted a church bingo game near Dubuque in the 1950s. When the Iowa legislature saw a new tax to collect, it whittled its morality down to an appropriate new low in order to fill the treasury. To compensate, however, it required each boat it authorized to operate to donate a percentage of profits to worthwhile activities in the community. The owners of the **Mud Cat** had given substantial sums to the historical society, a theatre group, and local Odin College.

Two friends, Tracy and Rhodesia, loved to visit the boat. Some weeks, they climbed aboard every evening, including Sunday. TV and movies no longer held much interest for them since the arrival of the boat. They would deny it, but the boat had become their lives.

Tracy was a moderately overweight forty-something who had divorced her alcoholic husband. The advent of the **Mud Cat** occurred about a year after her marriage broke up. It was a timely advent that filled, she gratefully thought, a gaping void in her life. The masses of people huddled around casino games and slot machines, the lively buzz of the crowd, the click, clack, whir, and bells of the gambling, the entire ambience, gave her a high feeling. She felt she had become part of the center of activity in Quinlan. She also liked the excellent food the boat served. It saved her from cooking and made the casino experience all the more enjoyable, all the easier to sustain.

Rhodesia was a slender forty-something, who had graduated a year after Tracy from Quinlan High. Her father had named her by randomly opening an encyclopedia, fingering the country Rhodesia (renamed Zimbabwe after the British colonialists had been forced out). He thought the name sounded beautiful and he insisted that the mellifluous word be his daughter's name. He bargained with the mother who provided the middle name of Anne. Over time, Rhodesia became known as "Rho-Anne" to her parents and classmates, except to Tracy who called her simply "Rho."

Rho was also divorced. Her marriage had lasted twenty-four years and had produced two grown daughters, one of whom, Jane, worked on the boat as a cocktail waitress. (The other worked in maintenance at the local private liberal arts institution, Odin College.) Rho got a special thrill of satisfaction when Jane served her a drink.

Rho and Tracy's lives became high drama on the boat. They became major players at a glamorous activity that saw them taking major risks with their money. This was supremely satisfying. To take a few dollars and try to parlay it into thousands was about as meaningful an activity as one could undertake. The boat offered the opportunity to take the measure of yourself, to see what stuff you were made of. They appreciated that the boat was always nearby. They could think of nothing else they would rather do than go onto the boat.

Tracy and Rho embarked on a Thursday evening in July. As usual, they planned to stay about five hours. The sun hung low in a sky that was just beginning to give a hint of darkening. They could see on the river a good number of boats and jetskis speeding up and down, avoiding the wing dams just below the surface that would demolish them if they miscalculated their routes.

They wore their Sunday best that evening. It was something they liked to do occasionally because it made them feel special, like they were really going out in style.

Rho wore a belted green dress that had a kind of Western-style flounce at the hem. She wore that dress regularly to the Apostolic Church of Eternal Heaven in Quinlan as well as on the boat. Both were highly important to her. The church met her deepest spiritual needs. The boat satisfied her most powerful psychological yearnings. Both gave her a mastery missing in her daily life, lifting her onto a higher plane of existence.

Though Tracy seldom attended church, she wore her semi-formal apricot-orange summer dress that revealed her tanned neck and shoulders, the dress she had worn on her last visit to church. She did not put the boat on a par with church. She was not religious like Rho. Yet, the boat had become the closest thing to a sacred place in her life. She believed in luck, that there was actually a goddess of luck, "Lady Luck." Since what you do and where you spend your money measure what you worship, Tracy, like Rho, could be said to be largely devoting her life and resources to Lady Luck.

Thursday evenings the boat offered a meal for a dollar in an effort to bolster patronage on one of its weakest nights. The repast was served on deck, weather permitting. The sky's darkening blueness was interrupted only by a line of cottony clouds in the distance. For July, the humidity was tolerable. The weather was cooperating for an alfresco dinner: spare ribs, corn on the cob, potato salad, iced tea, and beer, a no-frills hearty dinner.

Tracy and Rho looked forward to the late meal, mixing with regulars on the boat, and perhaps meeting new people. They felt the boat offered them a total package for their "entertainment dollar." Food, friends, gambling, a beautiful setting. The **Mud Cat** had it all.

As they went through the serving line, they struck up a conversation with their friend Marge, also a habitué of the boat. She had cut back her visits, which is to say her addiction, to two or three times weekly. This was a compromise, between having herself banned from the boat (which she had done several times) and going aboard every night.

Neither Tracy nor Rho had ever asked the boat to ban them, to refuse them admission. They had never felt the need to. They only gambled for a little entertainment and never lost control, or at least that was their publicly stated view.

Tracy preferred blackjack and Rho loved the slots. In order to stay together, they played blackjack first and eventually went to the slots. Tracy often pointed out that, of all the games on the boat, blackjack offered the best odds. They could invest any gain from blackjack into the slots. Often, Tracy's predictions held up. They would get ahead on blackjack, and fall behind on the slots. If they were lucky, they would leave a little ahead. Often they lost a little, and occasionally enough to make them vastly distraught at the pain the boat had inflicted on them.

Gambling had become a kind of occupation for the two women after Rho had won several thousand dollars on a slot machine. They were hooked, and they began to play more regularly, looking for the next big win, the next hit of casino adrenalin. They lied to themselves that they were getting fair value for their "entertainment dollar," a term they borrowed from the PR the gambling industry had concocted to facilitate denial.

Marge accompanied Tracy and Rho to the blackjack table. The dealer was a young blonde woman who emitted a piquant girlish charm. She lacked the hard edge and poker face that so many dealers adopt as their professional demeanor. They found this refreshing and they always gravitated to her game whenever they saw her on duty. She was one of the reasons their "entertainment dollar" was well spent, because she added a vivaciousness and sparkle to their evening. Indeed, she was part of their casino family, a kind of "dealing daughter," as they put it.

They loved to watch her graceful hands deal cards. She was an artist the way her slender long fingers with the artificial nails, enameled in pastel pink, swung into action, depositing a deft card to each player in her turn. And always there was the electric high-wattage smile that—once you had played enough against her—you knew to be genuine, offered because she enjoyed dealing to you and because she liked you.

Her name was Debbie. She had such great appeal that she drew many customers onto the boat, just to see her, to play at her table. Older men especially flocked to the baize-covered table over which she presided. One had even jested that he actually liked to lose money to Debbie since it helped to justify her being on the boat, with her scintillating, charismatic style of blackjack.

Marge won twenty dollars from Debbie. Rho and Tracy broke even. To celebrate, Marge suggested that Debbie join them for a drink during her break, and Debbie smiled her pleasure at the offer and accepted. They would meet in the saloon below deck near the stern of the boat.

Marge, Rho, and Tracy settled into the plump naugahyde swivel chairs, enjoying the whirl of activity about them. The **Mud Cat** had perhaps the best saloon in town, featuring a Mississippi steamboat-era mahogany bar. High, wide, sweeping mirrors with gilt rococo embellishment, walnut paneling, and crystal chandeliers conferred flair and a sense of authenticity. Mark Twain smiled up from the deep blue carpet amid other images of gamblers and ladies in period costume. Spittoons flanked the bar, and occasionally someone terribly nauseous from gambling losses (not to mention drinking) would vomit into them.

The spittoons evoked jokes. Usually it was a kind of gallows humor, for over time, no one beats a random number table (or frequent heavy drinking) any more than one evades death. Tracy, who enjoyed reading historical romances, imagined that those who witnessed the guillotinings of the French Revolution were endowed with a similar mindset. Both the boat and the guillotine stirred in the deepest recesses of the human psyche an uneasiness about the common destiny of all. Maybe it was why people had revolutions, gambled on boats, road jetskis, and had children–to defy that destiny for a while.

Rho beckoned her daughter, Jane, to their table. "Your usual, Mom?" she smiled.

Rho nodded. "Yes, please give me my Pink Lady."

Tracy and Marge also ordered pink drinks. They liked pink drinks. Drinking the sophisticated cocktails made them feel special. They could not understand why movie actresses did not spend more time drinking Pink Ladies on screen and less time smoking. After all, given the warning label on cigarettes about cancer, which behavior was more glamorous?

Once their drinks arrived, Rho asked her daughter, "Can you join us on your break? Debbie will be with us soon."

Jane smiled. "Sounds like fun." She glanced at her watch. "Lucky you. I have a break coming up in ten minutes."

Marge dropped a five-dollar tip on Jane's tray. She always felt generous even after a small win, and she wanted to please Jane's mother, her friend, Rho. Jane looked at the money. "Much appreciated," she said. "Enjoy your drinks." She winked conspiratorially. "The next one is on me." She handed all three of them a token for a courtesy drink and left to wait on another table.

A two-man, one-woman trio began to play. One man in a Country-Western shirt fiddled. The other, wearing a cowboy hat, played banjo. An attractive, middle-aged woman in sequined cowboy shirt sang. Some patrons got up to dance. Others cast their eyes about in search of a partner. The trio started with a Kenny Rogers' song. "You gotta know when to hold 'em. You gotta know when to fold 'em..."

Tracy stirred her plastic swizzle stick through her drink. "This is what makes it exciting, when gamblers take their break to drink and dance." For her, slaking a thirst was a good way to please Lady Luck. It was not only a social event for her, but a ritual in the evening's gambling. She felt she had to proceed according to a well-established routine if her luck was to have any chance at all of taking hold. Break from that routine and Lady Luck would leave you.

Rho put in, "I enjoy this place more than any other part of the boat."

"More than the dollar meal we just had?" asked Marge.

Rho smiled, "Yes. More than the meal or even the gambling itself. The people in this saloon, they top the experience for me."

Marge shifted her rotund bulk in her chair and slurped her drink. "I think I like winning. That tops it for me. But I like to dance, too."

Debbie joined them, pulling up a chair at their table. She stood out in her dealer's outfit of white silk blouse, garish red bow tie, black slacks, and stub-heeled black pumps. Her hair, cut in a preppy, and her lipstick a soft glossy pink, she presented a refreshing image of youth. At age twenty-five, she was indeed that. Still unmarried, she knew that some of the players at her table were more interested in her than winning. They wanted to win her!

Occasionally she had accepted an offer of a date, but few had produced a second date, and none had developed into a relationship. She had arrived at the firm conclusion that a blackjack game provided a poor matchmaking service. That conclusion served as a defense mechanism. Though recently made, it had already averted the substantial pain of more unpleasant dates.

"It's so nice to see you ladies," enthused Debbie. "I am having quite an evening." Her expression turned momentarily serious. "One guy won $800 from me. I hope you women bring me luck."

Tracy burbled, "You have arrived at Lady Luck's very own table!"

"We'll get you turned around," added Rho.

Jane appeared with a Black Russian for Debbie. She knew Debbie's drink and brought it automatically.

Debbie took a pull on her drink and visibly relaxed, sinking back into the deep softness of her chair. "I love this job. Best job I ever had." She set her drink onto a coaster. "Just to think, last year at this time, I was slaving away in 100 degree heat at the Quinlan Tractor Company." She waved her arm above a smile of satisfaction over the saloon. "The people are great! And just feel the air conditioning in here."

"What a difference a year makes!" chimed in Marge lustily. She began another refrain. "What a d f...," but Tracy put a friendly restraining hand on her shoulder that cut it short. Marge had imbibed her Pink Lady quickly and the latent singer in her had emerged. It required suppressing.

Tracy thought she much preferred the lounge singer of about a month ago who sang a medley of old standards including, "Lady Luck Be Mine Tonight." Marge could be such a ham when the bottom of her first drink emerged in view!

Debbie gave a short laugh. "I needed that! You're great!"

Tracy kept her friendly restraining hand in place. But Marge did not make a cue out of Debbie's comment, and the hand was removed.

Jane took a seat. Rho thought she looked lovely in her cocktail waitress outfit of short black skirt and white silk blouse open at the neck. Jane was a beautiful woman who had been very successful on the boat. Rho filled with pride each time Jane served her. Jane was the supreme accomplishment of her life, and to observe her at work was a special treat. She looked forward to the day Jane married and gave her grandchildren. Perhaps the boat would exert a less powerful pull on her then.

"Tips have been good for a Thursday night," Jane observed. "I am doubling what I usually do on a Thursday."

Rho smiled her satisfaction. "Excellent. You deserve big tips all the time. You're the best cocktail waitress on this boat."

Tracy raised her drink. "I'll drink to that."

Rho raised her glass, too, for the toast, and so did Marge, till she recognized her glass was empty. She set it down and her eyes searched the room for a waitress. She began to beckon with her free-drink token.

"To you!" toasted Rho, looking directly at her daughter.

"To you!" chimed in Tracy.

Marge sat mute, scanning the room for a waitress, frantically waving her token. Finally, a waitress came over and served Marge a second Pink Lady.

Rho opined, "Y'know, what this boat needs is a drink called the Lady Luck." She gazed at her daughter. "Could you suggest to your boss that is what you need. I'll buy it every time." She paused, adding, "As long as it is pink."

"That sounds like a great idea," returned Jane. "I don't know why we haven't already done that."

Marge was busy soaking up her second Pink Lady, but halted briefly to suggest, "How about a Mississippi Mud Cat drink? You can make that out of chocolate and booze. I'd drink it and it wouldn't have to be pink!"

Everyone at the table laughed. "That's another one we should've thought of," Jane responded.

"A Mississippi Mud Cat and a Lady Luck could bring in more customers," suggested Rho.

"Which means more tips, more tax revenue for Quinlan, more prosperity for all," said Tracy, who was still only slightly into her first drink, a libation for Lady Luck, a ceremonial drink to placate the goddess and the numbers she controlled. Beyond the ritualistic aspects of her drinking, she was a social sipper, not even a social drinker. She was attracted to the saloon for the social scene, not to get high. She had learned that, in a way, from her Jenny Craig diet class. Eat at home before you go to a party. Socialize at the party as your main goal. Stay away from the big

90

spread of beverages and food except to sample a few items very lightly, to facilitate conversation. She had applied the weight-watching dictums to her public consumption of alcohol. It had helped keep her weight down and she had never been publicly intoxicated, like her friend Marge who sat in her early cups at her elbow.

"More prosperity for all," agreed Rho. "The boat is good for my daughter and good for Quinlan."

"The boat is a good corporate citizen " added Jane.

"And a true friend to the community," hammed Debbie sweetly, flashing her electric smile.

A young man, clad in a colorful green-and-red summer shirt and charcoal slacks strode to the table. He faced Debbie. "Do you care to dance?"

Debbie liked the looks of the man and felt like dancing but boat policy prohibited it. Management did not want to get into the business of providing dance partners. That inevitably would produce a lot of ill will plus, possibly, a few embarrassing public revelations. "Thank you for the offer," said Debbie. "I appreciate it very much. But the boat policy is that employees do not dance with customers."

"I see," said the young man, a handsome fellow, thought Debbie. "I didn't know that." He paused, a bit pained, adding, "But thank you."

Debbie dimmed her high-wattage smile as he retreated.

Tracy opined, "That's too bad you couldn't dance with that gorgeous young man."

"Not really," Debbie rejoined. "No more matchmaking for me on this boat. I've had only heartache to show for it."

Jane observed, "We've found it's best to separate work from romance. This not like many workplaces where healthy relationships develop. Here you are only courting disaster." She glanced at her watch. "I have just enough time to tell you what happened to Shelley."

G. Louis Heath, Ph. D.

Jane told the story of Shelley, a former **Mud Cat** cocktail waitress. "Shelley went out on some dates with a guy she met on the boat. They had some good times together, and she really liked him." Everyone riveted a gaze on Jane, except Marge, thoroughly engrossed in her new drink. "It wasn't till later she got to know the real Earl."

"Earl the Pearl, I'm sure," put in Tracy.

Jane straightened in her chair. "Anyway, Shelley found out that Earl was the violent sort." She arched her eyebrows for emphasis and as an expression of dismay. "He beat her so badly after one date that she was unconscious for a couple hours. It got so bad that she felt she had to quit her job here and move to another part of the country. We don't even know where she is, and we—me and Debbie—were her best friends."

Rho put in, "You didn't even tell your mother this?"

"I didn't want to worry you."

"You have a point there. I would have been worried sick. In fact, I am getting sick thinking about the worrying I would have done." Rho's face looked stricken. "Is he still around, this Earl?"

"I see him around town every month or so."

"Now I am both worried **and** sick."

"I am not afraid," returned Jane.

"You should be," countered her mother. "He might attack you or Debbie as a sick way of getting back at Shelley. These guys think that way, y'know?"

Jane made a dismissive gesture with her hand, and turned to Debbie. "Can you help me assure Mom that we're OK here?"

Debbie looked sincerely at Rho. "He didn't date us. He has nothing against us. He doesn't even know our names. He might recognize us as **Mud Cat** employees. That's about all."

Rho looked relieved, but not completely so. A touch of anxiety remained in her intense blue eyes and uneasy demeanor. It would be difficult for her to look unworried. Her life had always gone from bad to worse, and she constantly worried about the "worse" that was coming her way next, whether on the boat or in larger life.

While Marge remained at the table to drink, Debbie returned to dealing, Jane went back to serving drinks, and Rho and Tracy resumed gambling, at the slots. They beseeched Lady Luck with every impassioned pull of the lever. They would not win that night, nor would their religion of chance bring them the "worse" they feared. They would pursue that tomorrow evening.

Rho and Tracy left the boat about two in the morning. They looked up at the stars gracing a velvety sky. A soft breeze whispered along the Mississippi. Several nighthawks, white bars on their wings visible, darted in and out of the swaths of light emanating from the boat.

Tomorrow had begun.

G. Louis Heath, Ph. D.

Barking Dog

Tim pulled into the restaurant parking lot and got out. Immediately, he noticed the frantically barking dachsund in a car at the far end of the lot, about forty yards away. The dog seemed to be defending its turf against him. Tim had never seen a dog in a car upset at someone at such a distance. It irritated him to be barked at for no reason whatsoever. The dog was barking its head off at him and no one else, just because he was there, not because he had done anything.

As Tim walked toward the restaurant entrance, the barking continued. He thought humorously that if the dog were looking for something to get upset about, he might as well oblige. He would get in front of that dog's muzzle up close and really give it something to worry about.

As Tim approached the car, the dachsund became very agitated. It stepped up its barking. It almost made him laugh to see how unhinged the dog became. It was like gotterdammerung and apocalypse coming together for the little beast. Tim's 280-pound monolith loomed into view and the dachsund went kabonkers. Tim made a broad challenging snarl, forcing the corners of his lips far back, baring his teeth in a mock attack. You asked for it. You literally barked me over here, graveling the hell out of me with your big yap, much too big for your sausage-sized body. You ought to have more sense than to provoke a big person who is usually easy-going.

Then it dawned on him, the dog was not so much aggressive as barking for help. It was 91 degrees according to the beacon atop Quinlan S & L across the street. In a car parked on asphalt with the windows closed, those 91 degrees created a literal oven.

Tim's heart immediately went out to the little dog, and he became very angry at the owner for endangering the dog's life. He wanted to save the dog. God only knew how long it had been suffering, barking for help. Perhaps it was close to the end now, ready to fall into a coma from heat prostration, yet continuing to valiantly bark for help till the very end.

Tim entered the Four Seasons Restaurant. He was both furious and upset. Yet he thought he had better find the dog's owner before he jumped to conclusions, before he assumed the worst about him. Perhaps the owner could not get to the car. Perhaps he had suffered a heart attack and was in an emergency room now. If so, he clearly would be unable to roll down the window for his dog or move the car. The explanation might be that dramatic, yet likely involved something less exculpatory.

Tim plopped down in a booth. He picked up a menu and opened it, but his main attention was on the other diners. He looked to see who might be the dachsund's owner. He also kept glancing out the window at the dog. If someone didn't go out to that car fairly soon, he would have to stand up and make a loud announcement regarding the impending doom of the dog.

Distractedly, Tim examined the menu, but he was too anxious for the dog, to be very interested in eating. He could only think of the danger the dog was in.

Soon, Tim could stand it no longer. Time to act. He slid out of his booth and walked to the center of the restaurant. "Excuse me!" he boomed. "Excuse me!" The heads of all the thirty or so diners swiveled his way, quizzical looks on their faces. Tim suddenly felt very uncomfortable standing in a restaurant, about to stand up for the natural rights of a small dog. How do I get myself in these situations? But, he felt it was too late to turn back silently toward his booth without saying a word. He would lose face if he didn't do something positive.

"Ladies and gentlemen," he continued, trying to force a smile. An attractive, middle-aged blonde woman seated at a nearby table smiled at him. He had to go on. He didn't want to diminish himself in her eyes. That would be utterly humiliating. He cleared his throat as he surveyed his audience. He hoped his clothes looked presentable. Leaving home, they were well-pressed and crisp. But the heat and humidity could have made them look already limp. Somehow he managed to push beyond his trivial self-conscious concern to the matter at hand, that of saving the little dachsund. "There is a little dog in one of the cars in the parking lot," he announced, "that is getting too hot. It is in the blue Crown Victoria parked just in front here. The license plate number begins with AY21. Is the owner in here?"

The waitresses stared disbelievingly at Tim. They couldn't believe he was doing what he was doing. And the owner looked none too pleased. He folded his arms across his chest, and tapped the carmine-and-black, paisley-patterned carpet in exasperation with his shoe toe, as he glared at Tim.

A thin middle-aged man in a floral-print summer shirt rose from his chair, carrying his glass of beaujelais wine. As he walked toward Tim, he sloshed a few drops of wine onto the carpet. All eyes in the restaurant were fixed on him and the little drama unfolding center-restaurant. One man commented to his wife how this was better than dinner theatre, and cheaper, too.

The thin man stopped a few feet in front of Tim. He stood there silently, staring a few seconds, putting everyone's nerves on edge. Then he said, "That is my Crown Vic you're talking about, and that is my dog Fritz you're complaining about. For your information, Fritz likes staying in the car."

"Your dog is about to die!" shrilled Tim. "You need to get him to a cool place right away!"

The thin man shook his head. "No way," he said.

"I'll call the police," threatened Tim.

"You do that and you have me to answer to!" said the thin man, who advanced menacingly a couple steps toward Tim. The man was much smaller than Tim who thought it ridiculous he was edging hostilely toward him. Maybe this was his umpteenth glass of wine and he didn't know what he was doing. No one had ever tried to physically intimidate Tim. He could in the past always count on his imposing size to avoid conflict. This character was giving off signals that a mismatch was of no concern for him. He seemed irrationally hell-bent on confrontation.

Tim was beginning to feel thoroughly silly standing eyeball-to-eyeball with the slender, underweight man. Didn't he have a wife with him who could call him to heel? The ugly thought occurred to him that two socially untethered, loose cannons were about to joust in the Four Seasons Restaurant because one was drunk and the other had overdone his sympathy for a distressed animal. He was discomforted by a raucous laugh and a few titters that emanated from the diners ranged about them.

Tim bluffed, "What will you do if I call the police? I warn you, I'm a lot bigger than you are! I don't want to have to hurt you!"

The thin man laughed. He took another sip of wine, spilling a little more of it as he brought his glass down to chest level. "Fritz is my dog. He's none of your business. I'm that dog's master." Tim thought the thin man spoke very coherently. Perhaps he was only on his third glass of wine and that had fortified him enough to extend a natural impulsivity into confrontation. That could be it.

There was a zealous animal lover in the audience. She, a middle-aged brunette in a green summer dress, got up and moved toward center-restaurant. She moved gracefully with a practiced ease, imposing a stabilizing presence on the situation, at least momentarily.

The diners had resumed eating, but they did not resume chatting. They continued to rivet their attention on the drama unfolding before them.

The woman positioned herself before the two men. She paused significantly, looked directly at the thin man, and said in an accusatory tone, "I have three dogs at home and I love them all. They're my family. It's important to me you treat your dog right."

The thin man seemed greatly taken aback to be so confronted. He stammered, "Well, I never, I never meant my dog any harm. Really..." His voice trailed off. The woman had caught him by surprise. He was at a loss for more words.

The woman returned, "If you didn't mean your dog any harm, you should've left him home in a cool place! You do have a cool place for him at home, doncha?" A tinge of crimson appeared in her cheeks.

The thin man nodded, but said nothing. All the confrontation had gone out of him with the arrival of the woman in green on the scene. It seemed to Tim that he was an odd character indeed, to have virtually charged at him, yet to have wilted so rapidly before the woman.

Tim spoke, playing the conciliator. "Let's introduce ourselves. I'm Tim. And you are?" He looked toward the woman.

"Gloria." She turned to the thin man. "And who are you?"

"I'm Fred."

"Why don't we all sit down together," suggested Tim. "I don't feel comfortable out here." A round of applause erupted from the diners as Gloria and Fred followed Tim to his booth. As they sat down, Tim asked them, "You don't have anyone who was sitting with you that we need to invite over?"

Neither did.

Tim was relieved that the attention they had attracted was dissipating, that the diners were returning to their conversations. He and Gloria could now deal with Fred privately, urgently. They had to get that dog into a shaded, cool spot as soon as possible.

Gloria took the offensive. "Fred, could you go out to your car and roll down the window? That would make me feel better about your dog." She paused, brushing back a wisp of hair that had descended over her right eye. "Then could you find a shady spot for Fritz?"

Fred stiffened but did not resist. He felt somehow in the sway of Tim and Gloria. They had a kind of power over him with their capacity to shut him out or include him. He was not sure why he wanted to hang with them awhile, but he did, and so he could not just walk away. He could only walk to the car and move it to a shady spot. As he was doing so, Gloria and Tim continued talking.

"That guy bugs me. He must be really bad, to treat his dog that way."

Gloria looked out the window at the parking lot. "His own dog must hate him."

"I think that is a distinct possibility," returned Tim.

Fred opened the door to his car and Fritz's bark changed from desperate to welcoming. The dog viewed the hot car interior as a fact of nature and did not seem to connect it to negligence on Fred's part. Fred, in all his callousness, thought of this as unconditional love from a pet. He was a prime example of someone who should not own a pet. Everything had to be his way and he anthropomorphized Fritz as a creature who loved "his way." No human being would put up with it for long, and certainly no woman Fred had known had ever endured more than two or three gauche dates. Every person he had ever dealt with had eventually objected, sometimes vehemently, to being treated like his dachsund.

The sun hung low in the west as Fred moved his car onto the street under a tree. As the summer day wound down, the exigency of the situation was abating due to the approach of dusk as well as the reparking of the car. It was an uncalled-for hassle to Fred's way of thinking; dachsunds don't live that long anyway. But to Gloria and Tim, Fred's action meant the crisis would pass. Fritz would not suffer a heat stroke this day. He would get his cooler, fresh air as the western sky became a band of azure and pink. They even imagined that they had been wrong, that Fred had true compassion for his dog. His leaving Fritz in the sizzling car had been an oversight.

Fred patted the head of his dog and let him run a few circles. He wished he could bring him into the restaurant so that Gloria and Tim could see how much he cared for his dog. As Fritz stopped to spray the base of a hackberry tree, Fred decided that, though bringing Fritz into the restaurant was unacceptable, it would be a great crowd pleaser to tether Fritz in front of the restaurant. All those people in there who had come down on his case would see he was a real animal lover. Maybe that middle-aged attractive blonde widow, or whatever she was, that had smiled at Tim, would come on to him. Maybe even Gloria would come on to him. Sometimes little things started big things. At age forty-eight, still unmarried, Fred occasionally still considered trading up from a dachsund.

Fritz raced ahead toward the restaurant, irritating Fred. He thought he had trained his dog better than that. Apparently some more training was in order.

He tied his dog to a honeysuckle hedge flanking the Four Seasons. He reveled in the smiles and approving looks directed his way as he gave Fritz another affectionate pat on the head. What an ice-breaker his dog was. This was a role he had never seriously considered for Fritz, that of a facilitator to help him break out of his shell and meet people.

Fritz strained at his leash and whined, but Fred ignored him and walked briskly back into the restaurant. Fritz followed his master with his eyes into the restaurant, then quickly directed his attention to the recent scent of another dog that had passed over the same swath of lawn. His nose worked the ground perfervidly, as several smiling diners observed his activity. Everyone was relieved to see that the little dog was healthy, active, and seemingly happy.

As Fred strode across the dining area toward Tim and Gloria, he saw that they had struck up an animated conversation. He felt a tinge of envy. Tim was getting to know Gloria when it had been his dog that had enabled the introduction of the three of them! He felt cheated. He owned Fritz, fed and cared for him. He ought to get a return on his investment.

Gloria smiled at Fred. "Wonderful you," she smiled. "You are a true dog lover!"

Tim chimed in, "Your dog seems so happy out there. Maybe the shorthair breeds don't suffer so much in a locked car."

Fred nodded and cracked a smile. "Fritz is a happy dog." He directed his gaze at Gloria. "I apologize for leaving my dog in the car. Thank you for bringing the problem to my attention. It was really thoughtless of me."

Gloria patted the space beside her in the naugahyde-upholstered dining booth. "Sit here, Fred," she invited. Fred's sliver-smile became a full smile.

Fred had another glass of wine. He began to really enjoy the company of Gloria and Tim. He even felt good imbibing yet another beaujolais after his new acquaintances took their leave of him. It was, he thought, a distinct advantage to have a cute little dog that enhanced your entrée into new social circles.

On their way out, Gloria and Tim saw that Fritz had put the hour they had spent with Fred to good use. The leather leash had been chewed in half. Fritz had escaped, and was nowhere in sight.

G. Louis Heath, Ph. D.

Silver Dollar

Professor Herb Nerd woke up that momentous morning with a strange taste in his mouth and a head that felt strangely heavy. The taste? Alfalfa hay with a dash of oats, surmised the good professor. Maybe even a little blue oak and eucalyptus browse thrown in for roughage. The heavy head he attributed to the wine he had drunk the evening before with his dinner at Rossi's, the best Italian restaurant in Quinlan. He had enjoyed a gargantuan repast of crab cioppino, tortellini, osso buco, a small wheel of brie, and a good dozen glasses of chardonnay that had caused him to slip on the foyer tile as he took his leave. Yet, certainly cioppino, tortellini, osso buco, brie, and chardonnay did not taste like alfalfa, oats, eucalyptus, and blue oak the morning after! Something was out of whack somewhere!

It was a mystery to Professor Nerd as he lay on his side looking out the window, lifting his head off his pillow repeatedly, and each time finding it extraordinarily heavy, a strain on his neck muscles. It wasn't until he had dragged himself out of bed that he noticed his hooves. Hooves! Startled, Professor Nerd examined himself and found that he had become a horse, thankfully a rather handsome sorrel with a glistening silver mane and tail. It was just as he would want to look if he wanted to be a horse. But, to tell the truth, he didn't want to be a horse!

In spite of himself, Dr. Nerd found himself rather striking. Before the bedroom mirror, he examined his tail, mane, and fine, light chestnut coat. "I'm a ten. Not bad!" he admired aloud, vaingloriously. But, after a few moments' reflection on what such horsiness would do to his self-image, he added glumly, "But I'd rather not be a horse! I'd rather be me, Dr. Herb Nerd, Professor of Philosophy and internationally recognized authority on the works of the immortal John Dewey, America's greatest philosopher!"

Sadly, Dr. Nerd's wish was not to be fulfilled. Here today, gone tomorrow, as they say, and tomorrow had become today, and the fully sober Dr. Nerd was today's horse. He knew this for a fact because he found himself carrying a rider in black cowboy shirt and boots, black leather chaps, and a black Stetson who was viciously spurring his flanks and threatening to cause him to upchuck his cioppino, osso buco, and brie. The meal had cost plenty and Dr. Nerd became quickly plenty twerked off at the prospect of losing his dinner. In protest, he jumped up and down like a creature possessed, kicking wildly, in order to try and unhorse the cowboy (who he thought might be the guy in the back row of his 8 a.m. class he had failed the previous semester). He fast became very sick and felt his beloved Italian meal straining to exit his gut.

The rodeo crowd loved Dr. Nerd's bucking act and roared their approval, provoking the professor into even more violent kicking. The crowd roared even louder. Professor Nerd was the best horse they had seen, an animal with real fire who was willing to do more than just barely qualify for the regular ration of alfalfa and oats. He wanted to browse the blue oaks and eucalyptus after the rodeo! He longed to roam the foothills, nibbling till replete, till he had to be readied for the next rodeo. He wanted to become a horse with special privileges. In short, he wanted to leave Iowa!

Professor Nerd did such a fine, frantic job of pleasing the crowd that, after a few seconds, the cowboy on his whirling-dervish back came flying off, hitting the ground hard. The vaquero had to be returned to consciousness with smelling salts by the rodeo clowns, and once his mind cleared, he knew he had had the ride of his life, that he was indeed very lucky to be alive.

While the clowns ministered to the buckaroo in black, Dr. Nerd, whose rodeo name is "Silver Dollar," decided to express himself to the crowd. Desperately, he wanted his fans to know that he was not a horse, but a Philosophy Professor, author of **The Complete Works of John Dewey Revisited** (Odin College

Press, Quinlan, Iowa) and **John Dewey Is Not Hooey** (which Professor Nerd single-handedly had published on an antique printing press in his basement, a press that doubled as his bed).

Silver Dollar, trying to communicate, commanded the attention of the crowd by rising on his hind legs and neighing loudly. The crowd's attention engaged, he fell back onto all four hooves and began writing in the dirt with the point of his left-front hoof. (Dr. Nerd was left-hoofed.) He wrote in large, two-foot-high, boldfaced Romanic-font letters. His message was simple:

I AM NOT A HORSE! I AM A PROFESSOR, ODIN COLLEGE. JOHN DEWEY EXPERT. RECIPIENT DEWEY SOCIETY AWARD FOR SCHOLARSHIP. PLEASE HELP ME! $300 REWARD!!!

Dr. Nerd started to specify a $500 reward, but he offered only $300 when he considered how he had been denied a salary increase last year for speaking out on behalf of animal rights. He had done so rather shrilly and had joined a campus demonstration against the research abuse of animals in the Biology Department. That demonstration had shut down Norway Hall and had gotten the college president, Stan Klemetsen, hopping mad at him. He would never forget Dr. Klemetsen's last apoplectic words. "Dr. Nerd, you are no longer my colleague," as if he ever were. "I'm ashamed to be on the same staff with you! You're a horse's ass, Nerd!"

At that, Nerd had cracked a fatuous smile and emitted a sound he hoped approximated a horse's neigh. The enraged President wheeled on his heel and walked off.

The President, he had to admit, had a lot of power over his life, but not enough to change him into a horse's ass with all the accompanying parts to make a full horse. Or at least he hoped so. There must be some mistake somewhere! He should've never had the waiter bring him that order of osso buco last night. No animal rights activist should have indulged in such a delicious dish of veal shanks braised with vegetables, white wine, and seasoned stock. Forsooth, that may well have been the dish whose zesty animal flavor, along with his guilt over eating it, in conjunction with the President's voodoo tactics (or whatever he'd done to inflict obeah on him), that had made a sorrel stallion out of him.

*   *   *   *

The crowd loved Silver Dollar's message in the dirt. They roared their loudest aproval and gave their longest applause of the day. They didn't like John Dewey because he had made it possible for their kids to roam free in the Quinlan schools and take over their homes with TV viewing. But they loved a horse lampooning, in the dirt no less, that libertarian socialist John Dewey who encouraged their kids to defy authority, shun work, get strung out on drugs, and in a gowed-up haze, explore and act upon the differences in their young bodies.

The big sorrel was great! He pleased the rodeo crowd in his funny, horsey, hoof-written way! He was a true, Midwestern, old-fashioned horse of another era who could really tell a joke.

As the applause faded, rodeo clowns and chute hands encircled Dr. Nerd and lassoed him, neck and leg. He had now become an equine behavioral problem that had to be removed. So they pulled the strenuously resisting professor from the competition area. As they did, the crowd rose as one and gave Silver Dollar a final round of applause. They only stopped well after their favorite horse had disappeared from view.

Once Silver Dollar had rested a few minutes, a pair of horny-handed rodeo hands began to resaddle the animal-professor in a mounting chute. As they worked, one asked, "Where did Silver Dollar learn that writing routine?," leaning his full body weight onto Dr. Nerd's withers to restrain the violently resisting intellectual.

105

The other hand grinned. "I dunno. I never seen a horse do that before. He musta been trained somewhere before he got here."

(Reprinted by permission from the Spring/Summer 2000 issue of **The Rockford Review**, pp. 50-52)

Fixing Minds

Andrew had had enough. They wanted too much from him. It wasn't humanly possible to install the new software in all the computers on campus in the three weeks remaining till Odin College opened for fall classes. Why hadn't they told him earlier, so he'd have a fighting chance to keep them happy? He shrugged. He'd give it a try. Anything was better than having his visa pulled and returning ignominiously to St. Vincent and the Grenadines.

Very early in the morning, he got into his new red sports utility vehicle and drove toward campus, listening to a cassette of junkanoo music. He felt he'd better get at it, even though the sun was just beginning to rise. It was so damn hot that an early start would make his work easier.

He parked in the front parking lot of the college that had employed him for three years. He shrugged. Sure, as a computer technician he could make more in the private sector, far more, but he liked the collegiate environment. Friendly, interesting, and till they asked him to do the impossible, not very stressed. Well, he was single now and he could devote all his energy to the new software. He no longer had a wife, and his two sons, aged nine and eleven, remained on St. Vincent with their mother. He had been liberated from the responsibilities of an immediate family for over five years. Being single solves all the problems, he thought. The current crisis was just another he could handle.

Andrew worked on a computer in the college lab for a couple hours and went for breakfast in the cafeteria. He loaded his plate with waffles and poured on a copious puddle of blueberry syrup, adding sliced strawberries and dollops of whipped cream. At age 38, he felt he was too young to worry about cholesterol and blood sugar levels. He needed to eat what he liked, what gave him quick energy, when he was working long hours to meet a pressing deadline. He dug into his breakfast, plying knife and fork with a body language that emitted a subtle reggae beat.

Two students, Phil and Dustin, walked over with their trays and joined him. They had been staying in the residence hall for the summer, working at jobs in town and each taking a class.

"Howya doing, Phil? How goes it, Dustin?" he greeted, taking the usual care to use their first names. As a small, intimate private college, one of the selling points was that the faculty and staff knew the first names of the students. Even if the student addressed was one of the misfits the college enrolled as it held its collective nose, everyone was required to trill the name as if they adored her or missed him. It was one of the reasons the college did well in recruiting and retaining students.

"Big test coming up," lamented Phil, setting his heavily laden tray down beside Andrew's.

"Same here," chimed in Dustin. "Need to do a lot of studying. Time is tight."

"Time management, time management," suggested Andrew. "Everyone has 24 hours in a day. There must be parts of your day you can use more efficiently."

Dustin winced. "We could've not gone out last Saturday night." He spoke in a pained tone.

Phil looked incredulous. "Study on Saturday night?"

Andrew smiled. "Sure, man. If you can't prepare any other way, you've got to do it. Sometimes Saturday nights must be study nights."

"That's asking a lot," returned Phil. "I don't want to have a nervous breakdown, y'know."

Andrew put his fork down and looked intently at the two young men. "I have an idea. I have software that has a time-management program on it. If you use it, you'll be able to get your studying in without being so squeezed for time." He did not tell them this was part of the software he had to install anyway in all campus computers before the fall semester began. He wanted to be regarded as a nice guy.

Phil took a bite of his waffle, savoring it, as Dustin agreed, "Yes, I think it is a good idea, Andrew. That might help." Phil nodded his agreement.

"The software is called College Time Saver. I'll drop by the dorm this afternoon and install it for you."

Andrew knocked on Dustin and Phil's door. Phil opened it, smiling sheepishly.

Andrew stepped inside. The room was littered with empty beer and cola cans, delivery boxes for pizza long since eaten, and clothes mounded in separate corners, waiting helplessly for a laundry day. He surveyed the disaster zone. "You guys need help in managing more than your time."

"I never could adjust after I left home," claimed Phil. "I've gotta adjust more to doing things for myself."

"Where is Dustin?" asked Andrew.

"I don't know."

That figures, thought Andrew. More grist for College Time Saver: locating your roommate.

"That's the computer over there?" Andrew pointed at something resembling the shape of a computer under a spread-out shirt.

"Yes. Dustin draped a shirt over it to keep the dust off."

"Well, man, move the shirt, and I'll put in the new software."

Soon after Andrew began work, Dustin appeared. He had been shopping and carried a plastic bagful of his purchases. "Sorry I'm late," he said. "Took me longer to find this stuff than I thought it would."

In a near-accusatory tone, Andrew said, "We think we found your computer."

Andrew observed that Dustin looked a little embarrassed about the disarray of the room as he put the bag down beside his bed and sat at the edge. Usually Dustin seemed at ease around faculty and staff. The untidy room may have exerted a stifling effect. Andrew could see very well how that might be.

Andrew continued to work installing the software. As he did, he could recall no room he had ever seen in his own college days that had been such a mess.

"Any of you guys smoke?"

He looked up to see them shaking their heads. "Why?" asked Dustin. "Is smoking so bad?"

"In this room, yes, man. This is a tinder box waiting for a source of ignition. You gotta be careful around all the junk you got here."

Silence. Dustin and Phil sat, chastened, waiting for Andrew to finish working on their computer.

Andrew went to the Dean of Student Life, Dr. Jeremy Sheldon. He was concerned about Dustin and Phil's room, that the residence hall might burn to the ground, beginning with their room. He had never seen anything like it. "Dustin and Phil are a danger," he warned.

Dean Sheldon sat back on his naugahyde swivel chair, smiling pleasantly, thinking of his golf game as he listened to the fifth or sixth complaint of the day about something or other. He knew how to appear completely absorbed in the complainant's concerns, totally sympathetic, as his mind floated over the front nine, delighting at the shots he would begin sinking in a couple hours. He would team up with the college president to play the business manager of the college and the CEO of a local company. It was during these games, with no faculty around to pester them, that they accomplished the most important business of the college.

"They are just kids," intoned Sheldon. "They are still growing up. Let's give them a little leeway, some space to grow."

110

"But they are nineteen years old, young men," returned Andrew. "We need to expect more, perhaps." Andrew added "perhaps" because he did not want to seem confrontational.

"But we do, we do," said Sheldon. "That's what four years of Odin College is about. Once they get their B.A.s, they become much more mature."

"A bachelor's degree means they can clean up their room?"

Sheldon discerned the acid in Andrew's tone. "And much more," he responded. He glanced at the wall clock. Golf was getting closer by the tick. What better life is there than employment at a private liberal arts college, interspersed with golf outings? Or, is it golf outings interspersed with bouts of "deaning"? (He liked to use the term "deaning" because it sounded erudite and technical.)

Andrew exited the Dean's office. He wished he hadn't bothered. Next time something came up, he definitely wouldn't bother.

Phil and Dustin heard that Andrew had visited Dr. Sheldon. They laughed heartily. "He'll never do anything," chortled Phil, "as long as our tuition is paid up."

"Poor Andrew should know better," added Dustin.

They dismissed Andrew's reporting of them to Dr. Sheldon because they liked Andrew, the man with the broad smile and kind daily words. He had pointed up what they already knew, that they had an animal-house reputation on campus.

They decided they wanted to end their infamy. So they spent a few hours cleaning up their room. When they found a pizza delivery box from the previous year under Phil's mattress, they knew they had made the right decision.

They entered their class schedules and part-time job hours into the College Time Saver program. Whenever they had another commitment, they entered that, too. After a few days, the planner had become a big plus in organizing their lives. The proof was their successful final exams in their summer classes.

111

In appreciation, Phil and Dustin offered to take Andrew on a country drive. Andrew smiled and did a few quick reggae dance steps. "Yes, man," he accepted.

On Thursday afternoon, Phil pulled his rickety Camaro up to Nansen Hall, the main building on campus. Andrew got in, noting that the car featured several dents and sounded like it badly needed a tune-up. He recognized it nostalgically as a "student car," a flivver held together tenuously on a student budget. He had owned such a car at the University of Iowa. He had bought it for $500 when he first arrived in Iowa City. It was cheap to buy, but expensive to operate. Before the academic year was over, he sold it, and began riding the campus busses. It had been folly for him to have a car. In Iowa City he didn't need one.

But Odin College was another matter. It was too small for campus busses, yet students had to get to jobs in the community. A car was a necessity.

Phil worked stocking shelves for K-Mart, located on the outskirts of Quinlan. Dustin worked in the Perfect Plastic Company's plant, extruding parts for a variety of toys. They were like many Odin students: They had to work to make ends meet.

The August day offered one of those overcast, sheet-metal-gray skies that hints at rain but does not deliver. It was hot and muggy as forecast.

Phil drove north from town toward nowhere in particular. Maybe they would stop somewhere for a beer. Cruising around was relaxing, even in a junker, as long as it did not leave you thumbing a ride.

Andrew liked Iowa summer days. A hawk circling over a cornfield and a kestrel sitting on a telephone pole, looking for a gopher or mouse to venture forth, provided a sight unavailable on St.Vincent. Perhaps its very unfamiliarity made it refreshing and, therefore, relaxing. Maybe that was it.

The inflowing air ruffled Phil's sleeve as his arm rested on the window frame. "It sure is nice to get away from campus. I needed this," he observed.

Dustin chimed in, "Living in a residence hall is very confining. It's not normal living in a little room. That's why driving around is important. I feel like I'm not confined out here."

Phil waved his arm expansively at the beauty about them, "Isn't it great? The crickets, the birds, the wildflowers."

The chirping of crickets and the songs of blackbirds and goldfinches in the fields along the road added natural C-sharp music to the bucolic scene. The luxuriant green along fencerows, stippled with Queen Anne's lace, purple coneflowers, milkweed, yellow vetch, and silky thistles, pleased the eyes with pristine, ragtag beauty. It was an inspiring, idyllic scene, a world away from campus.

"All of it really relaxes me," opined Dustin. "Takes my mind off things."

Andrew sat in the backseat as Phil drove and Dustin rode on the passenger side. Andrew was not used to sitting in the backseat. This is where his two young boys sat when he was still married to their mother. So, he felt oddly like a kid in the backseat. But, as large as he was, he did have plenty of room to be comfortable, and that was a major benefit. It compensated him some for being made to feel like a kid again.

Andrew was having a hard time fathoming why he had gone on this ride. He'd rather be tooling around the countryside alone in his new flame-red sports utility vehicle. He loved the bright red. He regarded it a true Caribbean color, vibrant and pulsating.

He had gone on this ride, he thought, because he was trying too hard to be a nice guy. He always flashed his bright, toothy smile and spoke a few zesty words to fob people off, so he could get on with his heavy daily work schedule. But Dustin and Phil read his smiling one-liners as an invitation to friendship. So, here he was, aimlessly traveling through the countryside, looking for that ineffable something.

Andrew felt offended having to talk to the back of two heads. He wanted to be able to react to the facial expressions of Dustin and Phil.

Phil swerved the car to avoid a row of three cyclists. "Those guys are a damn nuisance. Did you see that? Just as I come over a hill, there they are! I just had enough time to avoid them."

"It's a poor way to exercise," observed Andrew.

"Too much chance of getting creamed," put in Dustin.

"A few of them do get creamed every year," noted Phil. "They just got to be out here putting their thin little asses up into the noses of cars. It's like they want to die."

"Every summer hundreds of them take a week's ride across the State of Iowa. Four-hundred-plus miles. Crazy," said Dustin, turning for the first time to make eye contact with Andrew, who was pleased with that, finally.

The two young men began to unburden their problems with their parents. Dustin bounced his problems off Andrew, who volleyed them back. He smiled friendlily with each comment. He took pains to be polite. He did likewise for Phil.

By the end of the drive, Phil and Dustin felt they had made a true friend, a shoulder to cry on. As for Andrew, he vowed to stick strictly to fixing computers in the future. Fixing minds did not appeal to him at all.

Female Wrestler

Odin College stands like a lonely sentinel atop a hill overlooking the prairie in eastern Iowa and the small town of Quinlan just below. Founded by Norwegian Lutherans in 1901, it is celebrating its centenary. The fact that the tiny Lutheran college of 525 students has survived a century and, in the past quarter century, has progressed from a two-year A.A.-granting institution to a four-year college offering several B.A. programs is a testament to hard work, excellent strategic planning, a visionary president named Stanley Klemetsen, and sports.

"Yes, sports!" enthused President Klemetsen to Odin College's Board of Trustees, all twenty-five of them assembled in the recently remodeled, mahogany-paneled, crystal-chandeliered Thor Room in stately Nansen Hall. Just because we're in Division Two of the National Association of Intercollegiate Athletics, the NAIA, and draw little national attention, does not mean that athletics are less important to us than the Division One NCAA schools. For us, the term student-athlete is a very meaningful term." Klemetsen's voice rose sharply as he drove home his point. "The student-athlete role is an exceedingly important way we have of producing graduates prepared to contribute to society on a high level."

The trustees gave the President a hearty round of applause. After all, twenty-two of their number were themselves former student-athletes, mostly at Odin.

The golden, mid-afternoon October sun angled into the Thor Room, rendering resplendent the interior and enhancing the warmth and bonhomie of the gathering. "Though we award no athletic scholarships," the President continued, "our teams are important and they are proven winners. Our student-athletes have won the conference men's basketball title six of the past ten years and the women's title in soccer eight of the past ten years."

Another round of applause began, but Klemetsen cut it short by forging ahead. "And I want you to consider this. Not only have they filled our trophy case, their combined GPA is almost one-tenth a point higher than the students who do not participate in sports."

Trustee Rickey Yarborough raised his hand and was recognized. He seemed a bit nervous. "The grade-point differential is impressive," he said woodenly. "Students come here to play sports because they believe, as we do, that sports are intrinsically fulfilling and help us produce high-quality graduates."

President Klemetsen extended an arm toward Yarborough, nodding emphatically, smiling oleaginously.

* * * *

Each member of the Board of Trustees had been matched as a mentor for an Odin student-athlete. That evening, each took his or her athlete out to dinner. Ed Duncan escorted Virginia Finseth to the Prairie Dog Restaurant on the historic brick downtown square of Quinlan. She was the only female wrestler on the Odin wrestling team. In fact, she was the only female wrestler in the conference. As such, the 120-pound woman was breaking new ground for her gender, suffering the isolation and harassment that goes with the territory.

In defense of Odin, it was a very subtle, insidious harassment, something President Klemetsen and his staff were well aware of. Yet, despite their best efforts, they were unable to completely stop it. Klemetsen had concluded that his college could adequately deal with outright discrimination, but it was something else to take on the culture of male chauvinism.

The jokes by other wrestlers that Virginia was unable to get an intimate date any other way than through wrestling were never spoken to her face. They arrived via the grapevine, usually through other female athletes who dated wrestlers.

116

But, of this, trustee Ed Duncan knew nothing. He had no idea he was taking to dinner an embittered athlete who harbored a festering grudge against her teammates.

If Virginia had not been a wrestler who regularly defeated her male opponents, she would have been popular on campus as a moderately attractive blonde with a winsome smile. Instead, she was viewed as a "ball breaker" and a "bitch." Some even claimed she was a lesbian (a claim without substance).

As the only woman on the wrestling team, Virginia led a marginalized life. Yet, she knew how to cope, even thrive, in her fringe status. She had learned this from her mother who had once filed a sexual harassment lawsuit against her employer. Some of her mother's tenacity to challenge wrong and push on had found a place in her psyche. The daughter had become tenacious, a trait which helped her defeat her male opponents over 70 percent of the time. Unfortunately, the men took defeat as humiliation.

Though all this persistence in the face of adversity is admirable, it is not historically what young women look for in the college experience. They are looking for what the college viewbook and brochures promise, at least implicitly, beyond all the other stuff, and that is the opportunity for romance.

Virginia had entertained high hopes for romance, and her disappointment had contributed greatly to her bitterness. She had not wanted to become known as the woman who fought men in fierce, hand-to-hand combat. She had wanted a meaningful relationship with a man. Instead, by her junior year, the male wrestlers on campus had made a thorough outcast of her. In response, she felt they had a problem. After all, she wasn't wrestling them competitively, only the wrestlers from other colleges.

She told Ed Duncan about her woes over a pork tenderloin-baked potato dinner, easy on the portions and no sour cream on the potato, so she would not have to do any drastic weight "cutting" before the next match.

117

Ed was disconcerted to hear about her situation. He had believed that by coming onto the Board of Trustees, he was joining a PR-and-fund-raising effort, a Rotary Club-style boosterism. He was not prepared to hear what Virginia had to say.

Ed needed most the dinner to get into the mentoring role he had been assigned. He did not like it. Here was a heavier, darker side to being a trustee than he had anticipated.

Ed listened patiently to Virginia. He tried to be sympathetic. He tried to feel her pain, but he could not, for, at his core, he was revolted at the very idea of a woman fighting a man in ass-and-scrotum-grabbing fashion for advantage on a mat. This was not a conscious feeling. For the most part, it found expression in his vague unease over women participating in contact sports.

Ed was glad that his fourteen-year-old daughter, Debbie, had shown no interest in wrestling. The past summer she had taken tennis lessons. She wanted to play tennis in college and that pleased him.

Virginia Finseth soon left the Odin College wrestling team and went into therapy for her "violent feelings" toward men. Debbie Duncan continued her tennis lessons. She would eventually play for her Dad's alma mater, "Old Odin."

Odin College has recently completed a review of its sports programs. The report concludes: "We are especially pleased with the opportunities for personal growth that athletics at our institution offer the student-athlete."

Blood On The Needle

The view I have from my Odin College office is of a
graveyard. Most visible to me is a slope with headstones and one
30-or-so-foot-high obelisk, fingering toward the sky, the granite
attempt at immortality of a wealthy local family, the Bensons,
who buried the most notable of their lineage, Ben, in 1938. Or, at
least, this is what I have learned recently from reading the local
paper, Quinlan, Iowa's **Quotient**. I have been typing, and word-
processing, overlooking that obelisk for over 33 years, and only
in recent days have I learned that the obelisk was the Benson
obelisk. Over the years, I have rarely walked near or through the
cemetery, for it is across the street and no sidewalks run along
the cemetery side. So the place is not especially inviting for my
walks. On my rare intrusions into the cemetery, to walk its
meandering bituminous road, I never observed—at least I do not
recollect—the surname Benson on the needle-like monument.

But recently the obelisk began to catch my attention. A few
weeks ago, one night, about ten p.m. in my office, word-
processing, I took a swig of coffee and over the rim of my cup I
detected a slight movement on the obelisk, something
attributable, perhaps, to star-and-moonlight and shifting shadows
borne of cloud movement and the surrounding trees. I didn't pay
any active attention to this on that first swig, but at the next,
shortly thereafter, my attention became fully engaged. For what I
had fobbed off as shadow seemed to me on second swig to be a
person climbing the granite monolith.

Late on a July night, I felt that it could only be a kid doing a
kid thing. I could see how a kid could be challenged by a tall
granite monument, just because it was there, especially one that
looked impossible to climb without mountaineer's gear. The
thing looks very much like a needle at 300 yards, but it is
actually square, though tapered. The base is about three feet
square, the mid-section about two-feet square and the top about

119

one-foot square, surmounted by a pyramid about eighteen inches high. All this, of course, one piece of granite, an obelisk.

I became concerned. If a teen or younger kid tried to climb to the top, I could not see how he would avoid falling off and forthwith joining the population of the graveyard. I called the police and told them they might save a young life if they could patrol over to the obelisk in the cemetery. They said they would, and I returned to word-processing, forgetting the obelisk for the time being.

In subsequent coffee swigs I saw nothing further to engage my attention. I certainly didn't see any patrol car headlights slicing through the cemetery, though I could've missed them, as, like I said, I generally look up from my computer screen only for swigs of coffee.

The next day, I woke up about nine a.m. and I decided to take my walk in the cemetery. I hadn't been particularly thinking about the obelisk, the needle. A dream, unrecalled, or my subconscious, may have suggested the walk to me. For the first time in years, I would walk among the tombstones, amid local history, under the glorious trees that made the cemetery such a pleasure to view from my office. Certainly, I had hardly ever thought of death as I surveyed the graveyard. I most often focussed on the beauty of the place, admittedly, usually a sidebar to what I was doing on the computer.

I wore my Bermuda shorts, a short-sleeve shirt, and sandals, making for a comfortable walk. Usually my walks take me to places where there are people, living people. This walk felt profoundly different from the moment I entered the cemetery, for some reason or perhaps no reason at all.

Quinlan Cemetery is a place of life, despite its billing. In July, squirrels are particularly active, running across lawn and up trees. I have seen deer run from campus, across the street, and into the cemetery. But mostly what strikes me as so alive are the trees, a mix of evergreen and deciduous, including spruce, fir, and maple. The Norway pines are my favorites (as I am

Norwegian), a wonderful part of the canopy that confers wonderful shade on hot, humid days. Though the warbler migration is over, ending in early June, there are a number of permanent feathered residents, especially flickers, blackbirds, cardinals, and in early mornings, crows, who seem to have no respect for the dead with their raucous, prolonged chorus of cawing. It is as the planners of cemeteries had intended, a kind of affirmation of life blended with a certain denial of death.

A slight breeze moved the leaves, and the canopy seemed to have a real, independent life of its own, the canopy as a separate entity from the trees that comprise it. A kind of arboreal reification, if you will.

I felt good for a man galvanized into walking by a dreamy press. And it was like into a dream that I moved, soon noting the names on all the headstones I passed until I reached the Benson needle. **BENJAMIN BEAUREGARD BENSON, 1866-1938.** Seventy-two years, a full three score and ten, plus two. Not gypped, but not especially blessed by protracted longevity.

I looked for marks on the needle. Granite doesn't mark easily; that's why it is the stuff of monuments. I stood, I think a bit reverentially, and gazed up, thinking about my Social Stratification class, Sociology 331. The needle impressed me sociologically as a figment of stratification. Here lay one of the most wealthy men ever to do business in Quinlan, a timber baron of the late 1800s and early 1900s. Even in death, he stood above the rest. But in the larger philosophical sense, in the sweep of eternity, his efforts at eclipsing others by having a big rock erected over his remains seemed somehow inconsequential, futile, puny, even pathetic.

The Norway pine a few yards up the hill stood tall and beautiful, inspiring, while the stone spire struck me as only imposing in a sterile, intrusive way. To me, down in my gut and far up in my soul, it was also very offensive.

A couple of young kids, ten or eleven or so, came bicycling up the lane. They were chatting livelily among themselves about something and shooting water pistols at each other in a friendly sort of way. They came upon me as I was gazing up at the needle.

"Family to you?" asked the one in the blue baseball cap with the Quinlan Giants logo.

"Not to me," I replied. "No one in my family has the money for such a monument. Even if we did, we're all opting for cremation."

The other kid quipped, "Make your own hell, huh?"

I grinned and nodded, observing, "I think I saw someone climb this monument last night about ten p.m." I looked earnestly at both, moving my eyes steadily from one kid to the next.

"It's something we do," the kid in the Giants cap said. "We try to climb it once in a while."

"But we don't get very far," the other put in, holding up a fresh scab on his right elbow, "especially if the police show up."

I looked to the needle for a sign of blood, but saw none. "You got that scab on this?" I waved my hand toward the granite needle. "I don't see any blood on it."

"You can't," he said. "It's on the other side. That's where Phil holds me up, so I can try to go up."

"It's not possible to go up," I challenged.

Phil, agreed. "We're finding that out. Maybe last night was the last try. The cops showed up and we had to run for it."

"Maybe you guys ought to try bird-watching," I suggested. "It's easier, and you learn a lot about nature."

"Yeah, maybe," said Phil. "But there's something about climbing this big tall rock thing that is really rad. I mean, no one else does it."

The obelisk glistened in the sunshine angling in from the east. Every particle of it seemed lifeless, dead, despite the sun that flooded it with light, trying to get it to photosynthesize, like the trees around it. Lifting skyward lifelike, tree-like, a simulacrum of life-force, it is a betrayal of the natural lifescape. It offers no place for the eternal tide to flood in, nor ebb away.

"Who is Benson?" I asked, breaking the spell of the needle.

Both boys shook their heads. They did not know. But I could tell they knew I had been the one who called the police.

Born in 1866, Benjamin Beauregard Benson lived three score and ten plus two, his **kismet** to dwell under a big tapered rock that two teenagers would someday, recently, futilely attempt to climb. Wealthy, he was able to afford a salient kind of social stratification in the days following his physical death.

Arne Klemetsen, my grandfather, down the hill, a logger who worked for Benson, lies beneath a simple flat marker. No boys can try to climb it, though, occasionally a squirrel or robin scurries over it. The fallen leaves of autumn regularly obscure it, and the heavy snows cover it for months. Arne's marker enjoys a life of seasons.

The trees enveloped me with complex, ever-changing shadows as I walked through the cemetery, emerging at the street that I must cross to get to my college. A cloudless sky promised a hot, humid day. The cawing of the crows had finally subsided.

G. Louis Heath, Ph. D.

Corn Goddess

Some in eastern Iowa claim you can see and hear the corn grow by day and, if you are willing to sit quietly amid the corn, subduing your breathing, you can hear it at night, yearning toward the stars, moving incrementally but perceptibly toward the starry canopy and a stellar future as corn flakes in a box on which a movie or sports star smiles commercially for profit. These people are relatively few in number, but they are important, for they are the Quinlan Historical Society.

Some Quinlan, Iowa residents claim that those who comprise the local society that preserves the tradition and records of their community of slightly over 30,000 are a bit too zealous to be regarded as well-balanced citizens. Ralph Bitz, proprietor of the last family-owned corner grocery in Quinlan, Bitz Corner, argues vehemently with friends and acquaintances about seventh-grade teacher, Fred Mellinger, the President of the Quinlan Historical Society. "That man is just plain nuts! You can't see and hear corn grow!" In this view, he has a good number of supporters.

But the Quinlan local history buffs, led by Mellinger, believe that corn makes a subtle sound as it grows and that it grows so fast that the very process can be witnessed in real time. They are setting up a display in the downtown museum, a sort of diorama that will make clear how corn is seen and heard. Their efforts have begun to attract serious media attention, including a reporter from the **Des Moines Register**, which, if you are from Quinlan, is the pinnacle of all you could or would want to aspire to as far as media coverage is concerned.

The **Des Moines Register** sent Suleyman Jones to cover the Quinlan corn story. Suleyman, a University of Iowa journalism student, soon to enter his senior year in the fall, had landed a position as a summer intern that would enhance, he hoped, his journalism skills as well as look enticing on résumés he would send out during the next spring, as he prepared to graduate.

Suleyman deftly cornered his antiquated student-poverty-style Chevy around the sharpest corner on the approach to Quinlan, the one, he had read, that settled a decades-long legal battle between two farmers, surnamed Klemetsen and Swanson, who were determined to keep the county road off their property. The ell-corner was flanked by goldenrod, yarrow, and purple bergamot in glorious profusion. Then, unexcitingly, as he cornered the ethereal field of flowers, Quinlan began to appear in stark view. The four-story vacant department store of the downtown struck Suleyman as the most salient feature of the "village," as he cynically thought of it, growling the word as he sneered into the rearview mirror, his lips curled contemptuously. After all, he was from the cosmopolitan university community of Iowa City and he himself was a delightful international story, a Yoruba-speaking citizen of Benin who had come to the USA to study journalism, largely because his American father had encouraged him to do so.

The yokels of Quinlan could not be much better than the yokels of his home village in Benin! The further he got from yokeldom, the better. He could hardly wait till he worked himself into a premier journalist's position in Lagos, Nigeria or Los Angeles, California. He'd settle for either, far from the corn and yokels, the corny yokels who invented stories about corn growing rapidly, in detectable view of the human eye, quickly to the level of an elephant's eye. How corny. How yokel. How village-idiotic.

Suleyman cruised the corn-yokel downtown, past the miniature memorial wall honoring the several from Quinlan who had died in the Vietnam War. He noted that the downtown featured a good number of vacant stores and that the pedestrian traffic on the sidewalks was sparse. At least he could see the town dying, he quipped silently to himself, even though he would never be able to see and hear the corn growing.

After a bit of up-and-down-this-street-and-the-next driving, he found the historically correct, 1892 restored brick building that housed the local historical society and its museum. After he pulled into a parking spot, he stepped reluctantly out of his car. He had never before embarked upon an assignment he so thoroughly detested.

And, of course, Quinlan was worse than village Benin because here the provincials eyed him uneasily, even hostilely, because he was black, an anomaly in the ruck and run of their daily routine. Suleyman eyed the old brick museum building and the main street of the rustic downtown. "A person could get real lonesome fast here," he muttered to himself. Especially a black man. He shrugged. The word would soon get around why he was in town. The uneasy stares might become smiles, for he had heard that a good many, if not most, the townspeople felt, like he did, that Fred Mellinger and his fellow local history buffs were lunatics. In fact, they had become a bit ashamed of the opprobrium Mellinger and his coterie had brought down on the town. They probably wouldn't mind having the opportunity to express their opposition to Mellinger on the pages of the **Des Moines Register**, to show the world that not everyone in Quinlan was of the same mind, that at least some pockets of sanity existed.

Mellinger was true to his word and was there at the museum for his 3 p.m. appointment. He greeted Suleyman warmly with a jovial, "Welcome to the Quinlan Historical Society Museum. Did you have a good trip?"

Suleyman smiled thinly, nodding. He didn't bother to tell Mellinger that the directions he'd given him over the phone had gotten him briefly lost just before he had crossed into Quinlan County. But a journalist has no business twerking off an interviewee.

Mellinger was a portly, sun-tanned man of medium height whose summer shirt was slightly stained from sweat on a hot, humid day, the kind that make Iowa, with its regular summer rain, such an ideal place to grow corn. These conditions, Mellinger and his ilk were infamously boasting to the world, were so super-ideal that the naked human eye could observe the corn grow and the technologically-unassisted ear could hear it grow. "Well, this is it, what you came for, Mr. Jones." Mellinger waved an arm expansively toward the interior of the first room in the museum. "This is command central for our cause."

Suleyman made a special mental note of the term "cause." Apparently this man took very seriously a type of community activity, local history, which some could pursue passionately, but none he'd heard of—at least till this moment—had ever thought of as a "cause." "Looks good," said Suleyman, making sure not to inadvertently divulge his vast disgust with Quinlan and Mellinger. "I'm glad to be here."

Mellinger smiled. He wanted to speak to the press about his cause. After all, a cause needed followers and he was the leader, responsible for bringing others into the fold. He motioned Suleyman further into the first room. "The corn exhibit begins in the next room. One of the people working on it is around. I think she's in the workroom now. I'll introduce you to her when we get there."

The next room looked clearly like a work in progress, one not yet in any kind of shape for public viewing. But it offered Suleyman a rudimentary idea of the exhibit the Quinlan Historical Society was preparing. What immediately caught his attention was the exhibit case labeled **"CORN GODDESS,"** which Mellinger was very pleased to show him. "This is probably our best exhibit," he noted proudly, "the one most central to our cause."

Suleyman approached the exhibit, a puzzled look on his face. "It's hard to make out where this thing is going," he observed. "But, I can tell you, this is the first I've heard of a Corn Goddess. I thought you were doing an exhibit on seeing and hearing corn grow, a diorama that dramatizes how that happens."

Mellinger shook his head. "That's only our lead item, the stuff that catches people's attention. What is really important to us is the Corn Goddess."

127

"Doesn't Lutheranism work here any more?" challenged Suleyman.

Mellinger directed a severe expression at Suleyman. "It never did, as far as we're concerned."

Suleyman noted the rudiments of the exhibit abuilding. "Well, you've got a lot of dried corn on their stalks in there. It reminds me of a row of corn that died in a drought. But where is the Corn Goddess."

"Linda is in the work room," Mellinger responded. "This thing will be a tableau vivant when we're finished with it. Linda will stand in there as the goddess a couple hours each day."

Suleyman had begun to feel that this assignment had now become worth doing, not something to snicker at. "I can hardly wait to meet Linda, The Corn Goddess," he said brightly.

When they arrived at the museum workroom, they discovered that Linda had apparently left for the day. Like most beginning cults, the Quinlan Historical Society Corn Goddess Cult had yet to become highly regimented, though in the community exactly twenty had committed totally—mind, body, soul, and mortgage—to Linda, enough to even die for her, though not sufficiently organized to do so all at once, collectively.

Linda had become a symbol as well as a believer. Though it might resonate as the epitome of ludicrousness, it can be said that Linda believed in herself as the Corn Goddess. Though often unreliable, as she had just proven by her absence, she had come to relish her new role as a goddess. After all, how much more meaningful a role could an educated free spirit have? Perhaps her B.A. in Fine Arts from Odin College had prepared her for just this mission in life? Just the same, Mellinger wished she had stuck around to schmooze with Suleyman. That would've helped the cause. Clearly, before long, he'd have to make Linda more responsible. She had been malleable enough for him to make into an icon, but he had some more shaping, some more hammering to do. Even a goddess had to have an authority figure sometimes in order to stay the course.

Mellinger apologized to Suleyman for Linda's absence. He then gave a perfunctory, pre-packaged interview about the museum, the usual stuff he wanted in the paper. Plus, he began to tell the world about the new religion he had founded. "Our religion will have a tough time at first but then it will grow rapidly. The Corn Goddess is our prophet. She is not divine in our eschatology, but she does communicate directly with God. Only she and a few chosen followers, like myself, can do that. We have elected her as our prophet by a democratic vote."

Mellinger was somewhat abstracted from what he was doing because he was looking forward to the secret worship meeting amid the tall corn that night, where the properly proselytized could not only hear the corn grow, they could **feel it** ascend, as part of the deepest of religious experiences.

After slightly over an hour interview, Mellinger bid Suleyman good-bye. "I'm looking forward to reading your article," he said, as he cheerily escorted the journalist toward the exit.

But Suleyman was not so easily fobbed off. He knew a **real** story when he encountered one. He would, thank you, stick around and try to find out more about Mellinger and the Corn Goddess. Or else, he quipped to himself, he'd never eat another bowl of cornflakes.

Only a sliver of moon shone but the stars were out brightly. The cult members, in singletons and pairs, slipped stealthily into the tall corn of one of the cult member's farms. Silence prevailed, save for an uncoordinated symphony of widely disparate crickets and the soft progress of feet moving toward the night's worship. What had begun as an historical society task force on how to improve the museum had evolved into the magic magnet for twenty lives, the source of their meaning, a new religion. Who can say what engenders a new religion, but this one had begun almost randomly, and it grew because it seemed to fulfill a deep yearning, a basic almost instinctual thrust for something greater than the old, hollow, irrelevant faithways.

The silent, almost furtive silhouettes walked the warm, dark, rich soil, clad in dark to inhibit detection, carrying in memory the Corn Goddess songs and incantations they had, over time, as a group, written down as their hymnal. The divinity resided not in heaven, but in nature. God was in the corn, and to access the spiritual, the new group paid homage to the Corn Goddess.

Harking back to the nebulous origin of the Corn Goddess cult, some of the members felt part of it flowed from Mellinger's attendance, as a tourist spectator, at some Navajo religious ceremonies in the Southwest. After Mellinger conveyed his version of the Navajo corn ceremonies back to Iowa, and had for a couple years sermonized about their meaning to his followers, they were received as revealed truth, Facts Of Nature that took root and grew rapidly in the tiny group until they had developed a bible, belief system, and a rudimentary hierarchy surmounted by the Corn Goddess with Mellinger serving as her **eminence grise**. Anthropologists might term it "folk Navajoism," an example of "syncretism," and in the so doing, define a good deal of the truth of the matter. For, of late, aboriginal faiths have seemed to exert a considerable colonizing power, a counter-colonialism, if you will, as if to restore some kind of harmony to the eternal communion of men and women—the dead, the living, and the yet-to-be conceived.

Suleyman Jones followed the cult members, his mind soaring over the great story he had happened upon. He was thinking Pulitzer Prize, as he carefully placed one foot, then another, upon the prairie soil. He was thinking he wasn't doing too shabbily for a 28-year-old journalism student from Benin. He'd overcome a lot of obstacles to get where he was and now maybe he could take a quantum leap to fame and a job at the **LA Times** or **Lagos Star**.

As he neared where the Corn Goddess cult had assembled, he got down on his stomach and slithered military-style between rows of corn, his pocket-sized tape recorder attached to his belt near the small of his back. He hadn't come prepared for this kind of duty, so he would have to abuse a good pair of slacks and a new dress shirt, open at the neck, as well as a very good pair of wingtips. Why do we African ex-colonials have to over-dress for everything? he thought. Is it some form of compensation for being historically oppressed, or was it just him? With a glow of satisfaction, Suleyman noted that for the first time—and indeed, in a tension-packed situation—that he was thinking in English, not Yoruba.

He crawled silently to a stop. He heard voices. He unclipped his tape recorder from his belt, placed it delicately just beyond his head, and switched it on. The voices faded and he heard a rhythmic rustling, for a lengthy interval. Finally, Linda, the Corn Goddess, spoke. "I am the Eternal Giver of Corn. Bow before me. Praise Me." Her Voice possessed a stilted, otherworldly quality. "I am the Giver of Life. Make yourself prostrate before me." Suleyman surmised that she was reciting memorized lines from a liturgy the group had written.

Mellinger's voice cut in, "Hear the corn grow. Listen. Listen. The Corn Goddess works her magic on our plants. The miracle of Life is about us. We know it! We adore it! We worship it! Let us be in harmony with the Corn. All hold hands and feel the power of Corn."

There was an intense, protracted silence. Then the rhythmic swaying (or at least Suleyman inferred it was such) resumed in cadenced rustling. After about ten minutes, they returned to the call-and-response pattern of the worship.

The worship continued, in repeated cycles of rhythmic swaying, ardent words from Linda and Mellinger, and the soporific call-and-response. Uncomfortable on his stomach, Suleyman hoped the meeting would end soon or else something

131

interesting develop. He imagined that his tape recorder was becoming extremely bored recording it all. If it didn't become more interesting soon, it would never be Pulitzer material. If they didn't perform a human sacrifice and bury the deceased under the corn, he'd prefer they end their meeting sooner rather than later.

Suleyman waited in the darkness until the Corn Goddess and her followers had all left. He felt somehow different. The darkness now grasped him in an inexplicable, profound way, like darkness never had before. Until that night, darkness meant only the absence of light and the need to adapt with such measures as car headlights and flashlights. Tonight, the darkness meant something more. It was a mystery to him.

He walked out of the cornfield to his car. Driving by cornfields, the light from his headlights sliced over tassels and stalks near the roadside. He was no longer irritated at the lack of exciting events. In fact, his mood had become very reflective as he stopped at a convenience store for some corn chips and a couple bottles of cold beer.

He had difficulty getting into his motel room. He had to work the key a minute or so, before the lock released. Though very tired, he watched a little TV and ate. When he flopped on the too-soft bed, he fell rapidly into a deep sleep.

When he awoke, he did something he felt he had to do. He dropped to his knees, for the first time in years, and prayed. Every fiber, every cell of his body seemed alive, as if eternity were pulsating directly through them, as if life itself were a vibrant ecstasy and not a frenzied routine. For the first time, he felt a tranquility envelope him that was truly satisfying to his soul.

As Suleyman drove back to Iowa City, he felt he had been in the presence of Allah, of God, of a Supreme Deity. Tag it with whatever name you will, Suleyman knew he would never be the same.

*Meskwaki Burial Mounds and Other Stories from
Quinlan, Iowa, The Eternal Town where the Corn Goddess Rules*

The vast sea of corn whizzed by his open car window. Suleyman looked at the corn and smiled.

G. Louis Heath, Ph. D.

The Westward Mall

The controversy over the new mall had reached an ear-splitting crescendo at the county commissioners' meeting, which had sought "citizen input" about the proposed megastructure. Participating citizens had become uncivil toward one another, wrought up over their opposing positions. That it was a hot and humid day did not help, despite the air conditioning in the county building, which many entered withered and frazzled.

This was small-town Quinlan, Iowa, with a small-town ambience to protect. A substantial, vocal faction believed the proposed mall would destroy the best features of Quinlan, making it a hollow outrider to the new Westward Mall. Another substantial faction believed the mall represented progress and a better Quinlan and to resist it was a futile Luddite response to ineluctable global market forces that were making communities everywhere better places. Thus, intransigent perspectives were colliding.

Andy Martin used his turn at the microphone to argue against the mall. "It'll ruin our downtown business district." He extended his arms imploringly. "We have a quality of life to protect here. We need to stand up for Quinlan, not for developers who want to make a fast buck!"

The faction that supported Andy's view applauded loudly. The opposing faction sat as though chastened, waiting for their chance to strike back. Well over a hundred citizens were at the meeting, dressed casually for a summer day's heat. Rarely did a public meeting draw such a substantial audience. They had appeared because the word "mall" had taken on the connotations of "evil" and "good" for two separate constituencies in the community, adamantly opposed to each other.

Will Stern, a graying, tall, lean haberdasher, proprietor of Stern's Men's Shop downtown, spoke in support of Andy. He cut an imposing, sartorially resplendent figure, looking much like a senator in his three-piece pinstripe suit, worn in defiance of the heat, and as a sort of advertisement (his customary practice) for his store. His voice was thin compared to Andy's and people in the back had to strain to hear. "Stern's Men's Shop has served you for over seventy years. But we might not be able to continue doing so if the mall goes in. The pedestrian traffic and the auto traffic simply won't suffice to keep us in business. Face it. We offer service and quality. We make sure you're satisfied. Any clothing store in a mall will do far less of that than we do. I guarantee it." A small ripple of laughter ran through the audience. Stern's was famous for guaranteeing the clothing they sold. They did what it took to make an unsatisfied customer happy. Alter an item, replace it, or refund, anything just short of having the Sterns' attractive daughter sleep with the disaffected customer (though that option may well have been considered in a thorough survey of the options, so great was Will Stern's desire to sustain his family's longstanding success in business).

Randall Simmons spoke first for the pro-mall forces. He was a local realtor, a heavyset man who spoke forcefully. Those in the back rows who had been leaning forward to hear Stern, straightened up, confident that the volume was about to go up considerably. He presented the case for the mall, that would resonate in many subsequent comments. "Development is good because it is progress...The mall will rake in tax dollars for us all...It's a place to go when the temperature hits 30 below...The quality of our life in Quinlan will be improved." Most everyone had read his argument as advanced in the pages of the **Quinlan Quotient** many times over in recent weeks. Some were nodding not so much that they agreed, but that it was nothing new.

Simmons strode to a scale-model of the proposed mall named the Westward Mall. He deployed a laser pointer. "This is it!" he enthused. "Look at this beautiful building! I am so proud for Quinlan!" He proceeded to point to and elaborate on the inspirations of the architect, the latest construction materials, the tremendous view of the prairie, and the huge capacity of the parking lot. He sounded much like a preacher trying to convert people who otherwise were at risk of eternal perdition. Which was understandable because Simmons had been a Presbyterian missionary in Kenya for over a decade before opening a realty office in his hometown. He had saved numerous Kikuyu souls and he could perform the functional equivalent on the benighted of Quinlan over the issue of the mall. My mall is progress. My God is progress. Same argument. Move upward, indigenes and locals.

A wizened, elderly man with a cloth cap bearing the logo "Pioneer Seed," sipped from a styrofoam cup of coffee. His demeanor said that he was settling in for a long meeting. Others were also digging in, fetching their fair quotas of coffee and doughnuts, and pacing themselves with sips and nibbles toward the inevitable end of the meeting that would bring no progress toward resolution of differences but would garner those "public inputs" that politicians so covet in order to cover their backsides.

The audience was about equally divided between men and women—actually male and female, for there was one child accompanying his parents. He had moved a few feet from his mother, who was seated. He had devised a kind of game: he rolled doughnuts up against a wall, over and over, until they were no longer doughnuts. His mother didn't seem to mind this, or maybe she just hadn't noticed.

The maintenance man for the building took the boy aside. "Doughnuts are for eating," he admonished. "You're wasting tax money rolling doughnuts on the floor."

"It's my Dad and Mom's tax money," retorted the boy. "I can do what I want. I'll tell my Dad on you. He's the city manager." He drew a finger across his throat for emphasis. "Your head could roll for this."

The maintenance man apologized in a low, acquiescent voice as the boy began to roll a new doughnut. Hell, it was just a job. He had waited a long time for a good steady job, and he wasn't about to risk it challenging a spoiled boy about ten years old. He was still on probationary status, two months to go. Until then, he had no protection against spiteful, summary dismissal. He left the room, feeling angry and powerless, but confident of the wisdom of his action. He wished he'd never noticed the boy. Disarming kids of doughnuts was not included in his job description.

Before the evening was over, everyone got a good close-up view of the architect's model. All the refreshments were consumed or rolled into oblivion. And, the opposing factions had argued long and hard for over three hours.

As the last person exited, the city manager turned off the tape recorder and his son bounded up to tell him he had been bored the whole time. The city manager bent toward his son and advised, "It takes time to learn how democracy works. It's an acquired taste. Democracy, you have to learn to enjoy and participate in."

On a second-floor hallway, the maintenance man was just completing waxing a long hallway. He had the radio on low and was enjoying the eighth inning of a close baseball game.

G. Louis Heath, Ph. D.

Heavenly Music, Dying Wish

Unfortunately, it was legal, the music that the Quinlan, Iowa Apostolic Church of Eternal Heaven blared from its roof twenty-four hours a day. But, legal or not, Randy Junkins found it difficult to concentrate, hear, and sleep. The music was intended, he guessed, to proselytize him, his family, and all their neighbors. Yet, it was achieving the opposite effect of aggravating and enraging them all.

The man responsible for the booming music was young Reverend Sonny Sherman, a recent graduate of the River Jordan Bible College outside Elkader, Iowa. The River Jordan curriculum featured more music education courses than most seminaries. One course focussed on publicly played music to beguile the unconverted. From the course, Rev. Sherman had learned the value of mounting speakers on the roof of a church and playing the music normally reserved for those attending services. His church had long ago learned that, if you want to increase the flock, you not only had to speak the vernacular—English and its substandard variations—you also had to bring the message through contemporary music. This included rock music, and, for today's youth, the louder the better. So, Rev. Sherman turned the volume up on his Jesus-rock transmissions to the loudest possible setting. He wanted the town of Quinlan, much of which sprawled below the hill on which his church stood, to rock and, he hoped, absorb the message of his church.

Rev. Sherman was principally interested in letting youth know where he was and sending them his message. He had visited the "Field of Dreams" baseball diamond not far from Elkader, near Dyersville. There, he had thought: If I play it, they will come. And by "they," he meant teens, for he had learned at the Bible College that adults were much more difficult to sway from their religious commitments (or lack thereof) than teens who were ripe for bringing into his church. He wanted to use his strategic location on a hill to become known as The Church That Rocks.

He regarded his blaring music as a form of high-volume guerrilla warfare against the Devil. The Devil did his dirty work whenever he was not challenged. Rev. Sherman would use music to challenge the Devil. He believed he could drive the Devil away with loud rock music at the same time he drew in teens to attend Sunday services.

The pastor smirked inwardly. Due to his efforts, drug abuse, cults, and gang violence would diminish rapidly. All those were the work of the Devil. Fortunately, the Devil had big sensitive ears that could not stand rock music based on Biblical truths.

Randy Junkins detested Rev. Sherman's loud Gospel-rock music. He had phoned the pastor, who refused to lower the volume. "This is all very legal," Rev. Sherman had retorted sanctimoniously. "I am within my rights here. I can spread the Gospel this way."

Randy told him to go to hell and slammed the phone down. He next called city hall. "Our cat can't even go to sleep," he complained to the city manager who told him that, lamentably, Rev. Sherman was indeed acting legally, something that he and his own family, who also lived within earshot of the church, deeply regretted and resented.

"We need to get a new ordinance passed to make Rev. Sherman's music illegal," suggested Randy.

"I am drafting an ordinance now," returned the city manager. "But it could take up to three months before the council voted on it, and then there is no guarantee it will pass. There are some very liberal free-speech advocates on the council. They might view Rev. Sherman's music as free speech. In fact, that's the way the law views it now."

"I see, I see," intoned Randy. "So I have a good three months to endure this blaring music?"

"Regrettably, that might well be the case."

Bleary-eyed Randy felt depressed as he hung up. How were he and his family to stand the horrific music for three more months? Or more! Three more days would be bad enough. He turned to his wife, Flo. "I could maybe tolerate 'Ave Maria,' whether by Gounod or by Schubert I wouldn't care. But his high-decibel rock stuff has got to go!"

"I feel ten years older," chimed in Flo furiously. "Between driving the kids to ball games and the pool, grocery shopping, and running all the other errands, that boom-boom church on the hill, has just drained me. I'm frazzled. I'd like to slug that preacher guy Sherman in his kisser!"

"Maybe that's just what we'll do, slug him in the kisser," offered Randy. "That may not stop the music, but it'll make me feel a lot better about myself, that I had done something to stand up to the guy."

Flo nodded, then shook her head, as if she were catching herself, stopping from doing something that went against the grain. "It'd make us feel better, maybe, but it wouldn't accomplish anything. Besides, we've never done anything violent in our entire lives. We won't start now, that's for sure! We need to do something that conciliates, that resolves the situation."

Randy's eyes lit up. "Remember that peacemaking class we took in college, when we were juniors. I still have the textbook. Maybe we can get some ideas from that."

Flo flicked back her flowing brown hair. "I remember. Why haven't we thought of that before? Dr. Baldwin said he hoped we'd apply what we learned in his class after we graduated."

Randy sighed heavily. "We've never run into such an adamant true believer before. That's why we haven't thought about using peacemaking, till now. This guy won't give us any space for conflict resolution. We've got to find a way to make peace."

"I remember stuff on Gandhi and A. J. Muste in that book, and all the other great pacifists we studied," observed Flo. "Maybe we can draw some insights from them."

"Yes. We're not gangbangers that slug or shoot it out. We can do better than clobber Rev. Sonny Sherman in the kisser, though the very idea can't help but have some appeal," Randy smiled. "We'll try to find a way to make both Sonny and ourselves better people. Maybe peacemaking will do that for us."

Flo saw a purple finch land on the bird feeder at the kitchen window. The creature seemed so happy, so natural, so complete. Its song of C-sharps was a paean to the joys of nature, as opposed to the conflicts of man. Flo thought that wherever men and women intrude on nature to build permanent residences and establish towns and cities, the rhythms and satisfactions of nature begin to lose out. Maybe that was what was happening to Rev. Sherman and themselves. Their living in stultifying, ticky-tacky houses in close proximity had disrupted the cadence and flow that their lives should have, and set them up for inevitable conflict and disappointment.

Perhaps Rev. Sherman had as much right as the purple finch to offer his music to the world? She paused in thought. But that was for Rousseau's world, uninhibited by civilization. She and Randy were dealing with a crowded world that had turned in on itself. Rev. Sherman had no right to diminish their lives!

Yet, Flo posed the hypothetical question to her husband. "D'you suppose that Rev. Sherman has the same right to send music into the world as that finch?"

Randy smiled thinly, "I wouldn't go that far, but looking at that question may help us with the peacemaking process, somehow."

Flo nodded in agreement.

Randy and Flo went through their old college peacemaking text over the next few days, scouring it for hints as to how to deal with the loud music. What gravelled them especially was that the incessantly booming music made it difficult for them to read up on how to make peace with the man responsible for the aggravation. That presented a special irony for them, but they read on, talked on, thought on. They consoled themselves: Gandhi and Muste had both spent long periods in prison in the service of peace. Maybe they could suffer a little, too, in their own way, trying for peace.

It shouldn't be that difficult to address the soul and humanity of a pastor, they thought. After all, souls were literally his business. He was no Hitler or Stalin. But how to get beyond the intransigence and bluster? How to make unreason give way to reason, cause inconsiderateness to make way for courtesy? The devil was always in the details! The task of the peacemaker was never easy.

Certainly, they would have to meet with Rev. Sherman, but to go back to face-to-face harangues with the man would only exacerbate the situation. To avoid that, they needed a mediator, a third party that they and Sherman trusted.

"Who could help us?" asked Flo, almost rhetorically, after they had been trying to come up with the right person for over an hour.

Randy sat back in his chair in the study where they were brainstorming the matter, as per the old text's suggestion. "Someone from our church," he threw out. "Someone from their church."

"No, no. Our church and their church are not neutral."

"At least they can't be **perceived as neutral**," noted Randy, emphasizing a phrase from the text. "We need to find someone who can be **perceived** as not being biased for or against one side or the other." He lightly rapped his knuckles against his forehead. "But who? Who can both sides trust?"

Suddenly, Flo's face came alive with a bright idea. "How about someone randomly selected from the phone book? How can it get any fairer than that?"

"That's a great idea!" enthused Randy. "How can Rev. Sherman object to that?"

Randy phoned the pastor and offered his idea. Rev. Sherman, who had taken a basic statistics course in college, knew that the work of randomness most always keeps the Devil at bay. So, he agreed, as long as some of his congregation could witness the drawing of the name, to make sure it was really random. Randy could see nothing wrong with that, and they agreed to meet at Sherman's church the next evening at seven o'clock.

When Randy and Flo arrived at the Apostolic Church of Eternal Heaven, they were escorted into the large chapel. To their surprise, the place was virtually full as if it were a regular service. Rev. Sherman had decided to make a big to-do of the drawing, to use it to bond his congregation even closer to him, and to extend their sense of mission as he envisioned and directed it. If the mission was to be modified by a randomly selected mediator, who, obviously, would be a random surprise, he sought to cover his backside by closely involving his flock, as witnesses and spectators.

As Randy and Flo walked down the aisle to the front of the church, they could not help but resent the surprise that had been sprung on them. They had made the mistake of thinking that Rev. Sherman would make a low-key affair of the drawing, with a witness or two from his church. When he asked to bring witnesses, they should have been leery, asking how many he would bring, and announcing their intention to bring their own.

As they approached the altar, they noted the unusual Jesus-rock-band section flanking one side of the pulpit. On the other, stood a large full-body immersion tank of stainless steel encased in a mahogany frame. What a loud ritual that must be, baptism accompanied by a bassist, keyboardist, and the rest of a pulsating band.

143

In the past, the church had presented Amy Grant or Michael Bolton-style Christian pop-rock bands or recordings. The congregation liked that musical fare. But lately, Rev. Sherman had left that mainstream evangelical-fundamentalist music behind in favor of much more strident, high-decibel stuff. That is where the trouble had begun, with that change, when that new music no longer was contained within the reverberating walls of the church and after it had begun to electronically harass the very nerve and brain cells of those within a wide range.

Rev. Sherman stepped forward and shook the hand of Randy, then Flo. "I'm ready. We're ready for the big drawing," he announced matter-of-factly. He waved them toward the baptismal tank, escorting them to the side of it. He peered down. "See those pieces of paper. That's the phone book cut up, one slip for every person."

"Do you want to get down in there and double-check to see what I say is true?"

Flo and Randy exchanged glances. Neither of them wanted to get in the tank and scrabble about to see if the names were all different. "It'd've been better if you had let us cut up the phone book with you and join you in tossing the names in," said Randy, surveying the stained glass and rafters of the church. "But this is a church, and if your congregation certifies it's fair, we'll go along."

Rev. Sherman turned his corpulent bulk toward his congregation. "Was it fair?" he asked.

Various voices were raised, testifying that the phone book had been cut up name by name, and the names dumped into the tank. Two phone books had been required to avoid two names on one slip. For each slip, one side had been blackened to cover a name. It sounded to Flo and Randy like the drawing would be fair.

It did occur to them, however, that randomly selecting one of the twenty-six letters of the alphabet and then randomly selecting a number, counting down that far into the C's, P's, or whichever letter in the phone book, to produce a mediator, would have been less of a hassle. But, for the sake of peacemaking, they were willing to let Rev. Sherman make a church extravaganza of the process.

A small boy stepped forward. Rev. Sherman intoned a solemn blessing and put a blindfold on the boy, who lowered himself into the tank and sifted through the slips of paper for a long time, a good three or four minutes, as the pastor prayed loudly over him. Finally, the boy, no more than six or seven years old, held up a slip for Rev. Sherman to take.

The pastor examined the slip, and looked up, clearing his throat. There was total silence. A palpable sense of expectation and significance held sway over everyone, as though any motion or sound would be a kind of heresy. Holding out the slip so that Flo and Randy could read and verify it first, he moved it back into his direct line of vision and announced, "The winner is Elmer Adner, P. O. Box 69, rural Quinlan."

The congregation erupted into applause, as they exchanged puzzled glances. Who had ever heard of Elmer Adner? Offhand, no one seemed to. Some thought he might be a farmer. Others speculated a retiree. If he worked in town, someone would've known about that. So, that identity was excluded.

Elmer Adner, aged ninety-six, was a retired railroad conductor from another part of the state who had lived in an inherited farmhouse sixteen miles outside Quinlan the past thirty years. His wife had died twenty-six years ago. His current companion was a stray calico cat he had adopted. He moved about with the aid of a walker, and never left home except for an occasional ride in the Quinlan Agency On Aging's van.

Elmer would die in three days. His dying wish was that the Apostolic Church of Eternal Heaven limit its alfresco playing of music to two evenings each week, an hour each time, and that the music be that of Amy Grant and Michael Bolton, whose CDs he listened to regularly.

145

Rev. Sherman stood at Elmer's bedside as he expired. He had given his word he would carry out his deathbed wish. And he did.

Deer Blood

Allison Hahn thumbed through the pages of the **Quinlan Quotient**, looking for the **Find-A-Date** section. Divorced over a year, she had been trying for some time to find a man to date long-term. Her social network had not produced an acceptable man, nor had her workplace, the Iowa Department of Human Services, where she was a social worker.

She had had some dates in the year since her divorce, but her dates had proved at best minimally satisfactory. She had only once proceeded to a second date, never a third. She knew social science research advised that the best results were obtained by drawing on personal networks, where the reputation of a man was well-known. Friends and colleagues can help screen out bad matches.

She knew that date-seekers writing thirty or so words for a newspaper were often offering what it took to elicit interest more than they were telling the truth. Accordingly, she was appropriately leery. Yet, she felt, at the moment, she had no alternative to using **Find-A-Date**.

Allison scanned the many entries listed under **"Men Seeking Women"** till she saw personal ad number 77: **"DWM, professional, middle-aged, father of two boys in college. Master's degree. From Minnesota. Recently moved to Quinlan. Wants to meet college-educated woman, 32-45. Non-smoker. Social drinker acceptable."**

Allison liked that ad. Few personal ads listed a college education or professional status. This guy, she thought, might not become her Mr. Wonderful, but at least he had some credentials that put him in the same social class. She decided to invest a few dollars and listen to his taped message at the phone number listed at the top of the newspaper page that featured **"Find-A-Date."**

147

The recording was encouraging. "Glen" was a divorced 44-year-old who had moved to Quinlan to teach the seventh grade a year ago. He had taught in Shakopee, Minnesota for twenty years. With his sons in college, and single again, he wanted to begin a new life, and that meant for him a new job, in a new school, in a new town. He had found Quinlan by reading a classified ad in a Minneapolis paper describing the teaching position he would soon fill.

Glen talked a lot. His taped message ran for eight minutes. At three dollars a minute, talk was not cheap. Yet, Allison felt she garnered a good candid glimpse of Glen. She liked the sound of his voice. There was something genuine and comforting about it. Nothing in it fed her fears about **Find-A-Date** listings.

Allison left a message for Glen, telling a little about herself and saying she hoped very much to hear from him. It was late Saturday night and she expected to hear from him the next day, or the day after, if she heard from him at all.

Sunday afternoon, Allison took a walk through the downtown park. The city garden had begun its brilliant spring efflorescence. The tiny yellow flowers of the coreopsis hunkered beneath the large honey-golden rudbeckia flowers. Mat daisies, anacyclus, hugged the troweled earth while the purple hibiscus blossoms soared over four feet high. The flowers offered a splendid May vista of yellow, gold, white, and purple. She drank it all in, eyes wide to the continuum of color.

Robins scratching for worms in the garden and red squirrels flicking their tails nervously as they romped over grass and up trees added to her sense of vernal renewal. Her domestic life may have ended, leaving her looking for a new life. Yet, the joys she found in the natural world had not diminished.

Allison walked around the park's small lake, the surface rippled gently by breezes. She thought of Glen. Did he smile thinly or toothily? Was he a gentle person or someone for whom the violence of sports appealed? Was he balding? He didn't say anything about his hair. At forty-four, he could already be cue-ball bald! She did not want a bald man any more than he wanted a smoker. She didn't smoke. He'd have to have hair.

She finished her turn around the blacktop path that circled the lake and headed for home, looking up at a pale blue sky with a few fluffy white clouds on the horizon. They held no hint of rain, nothing to disrupt a day. If Glen called, they could maybe even meet that evening. The weather would not be a factor.

Allison thought that she should not construct a Glen who existed only in her imagination. She must guard against that, for this was the very unreal world that made Harlequin and Silhouette romances sell so spectacularly. Though she had read several books of this escapist fare, she saw through them, to their unhealthy denial of the real world of women. As a social worker, she dealt regularly with the sad outcomes of such denial, usually a woman who refused to leave a violent man. She would not be deluded by fantasies.

Allison found no message from Glen on her answering machine. Mildly disappointed, she proceeded to prepare a dinner for one that she wished could be for two. She listened to the local pop-music station that played the old standards, the "classics" as the deejay termed them. Once a popular song is five years old, she thought, it becomes a "classic." It seemed to her that the very word classic had lost any semblance of true meaning to those in their teens and early twenties who spent an inordinate amount of time listening to the music that she now listened to pleasurably as she cooked.

She stood at the stove, steaming broccoli and carrots, as the final entrée of her dinner. She speculated as to what Glen's last name might be. He had been in Quinlan a year but their social circles had never intersected. She laughed. A failure of social circles. That's why he had to place an ad in the paper!

The radio blared a Shania Twain song for the third time in a half-hour. Allison strode purposely to the shelf on which it sat and switched it off. She liked Shania's songs, almost as much as some much younger, but Shania had begun to pall.

The absence of music felt great, an unusual sensation. Why did she even listen to the radio? It flashed to her that it was an unwanted habit from her previous married life. She absorbed the enveloping quiet and felt a suffusing warmth within. Her mind floated high above the welter of social problems she had encountered the previous week at the Department of Human Services. It was the first complete peace of mind she had enjoyed since last Sunday.

She prayed silently before eating, and in silence, almost reverentially, she ate. The whitefish, carrots, broccoli, and sourdough bread seemed to activate her tastebuds more than usual. Maybe everything was more energized in silence. Numerous religious orders had been founded on that premise. She had not realized she missed silence so much. Her life had been until recently the very loud noise of two daughters and a husband, and, as always, her social work job. Now that her two daughters were in college and her husband gone, she imbibed silence as if she were on a sizzling desert and quaffing her first water in days. She had under-appreciated the healing power of silence. She was realizing that her weekends could be totally silent, if she wished.

She cleaned up the table and washed the dishes. As she finished, the phone rang. She crossed the kitchenette to the phone. "Hello," she said cheerily.

A husky voice spoke. "This is Glen Morrison. You left a message at **Find-A-Date** for me. I am returning your call."

"Thank you," responded Allison. "I was hoping you would call."

There was a short, slightly uneasy silence. She glanced at her watch: 6:49 p.m. As she dropped her arm to her side, he resumed speaking and she sat down. "I want to tell you how pleased I am that you called. It's hard to know where to begin, but let me start by asking, what can I tell you about myself that you don't already know? Do you have any questions?"

"You have two sons, you said on your tape. Tell me about them." She paused, and before he had a chance to speak, added, "I have two daughters. The experience of two sons seems so very different, I'd like you to tell me what the best thing and the worst thing that have happened in raising them."

Glen muttered something inaudible, then observed, "That is a very tough question. I don't know if I could right off the top of my head come up with the best and the worst. But, I can give you one example of the good and one example of the bad I've experienced in raising them."

"That would be wonderful," returned Allison.

The bad was the time his eldest son was severely injured in an auto accident. He had required lengthy hospitalization and occupational therapy. The good happened when his youngest son and his high school basketball team made it to the Minnesota State 3-A Championship Game, winning by a point in overtime. His son's jump shot from the lane had provided the margin of victory.

As he spoke, Allison noted how he defined bad and good in terms of events. He did not recount his feelings. She did not like that. Her ex-husband never could convey his feelings to her, an inadequacy that had contributed to the misery and ultimate collapse of their marriage. Maybe Glen was that way, too.

They arranged a date for Tuesday evening. They would drive up to Lake Meskwaki and have dinner in the chalet-style restaurant overlooking the lake. Allison looked forward, guardedly, to the drive and dinner. She had been disappointed before. A blind date arranged through **Find-A-Date** could only multiply the usual risk involved in a first date. But she had to be optimistic. Otherwise, her **Find-A-Date** leap of faith would be unthinkable.

At five p.m. Tuesday, Allison rushed home from work and dressed for the date in a bright green summer dress and sandals. A little late, Glen appeared at the door. He knocked rather than press the doorbell button, an event she stored in her mental-tickler file. Maybe he hadn't even seen it, she conjectured.

At the sight of him, Allison was relieved. All systems were still go. Glen was not bald! She could see a full head of luxuriant brown hair, a shock of which hung over an eyebrow. "I had a hard time finding your place," he smiled as she opened the door.

"Sorry about that," she smiled back. "What was the problem?"

"I mistook sixth avenue for sixth street. I found out the hard way there is no 2315 sixth street. Good thing I started out early." He glanced at his watch. "Sorry, I'm eight minutes late."

"No problem," she said. She knew the Quinlan streets were tricky that way, even if one had lived here for years. Even long-time residents found their way to new addresses using a city map.

Glen liked her street, lined with many silver maples. He referred to it as "maple-embowered." He felt it epitomized the Normal Rockwell image of a small Midwestern town. She had never thought of it that way. She knew only that it was a beautiful shady street and every walk on it was a walk in beauty.

Glen was a portly fellow, about five-foot-eight, about an inch taller than Allison. He wore a lime-green guyabera shirt, gray dress slacks, and penny loafers. He twisted his car key end over end in his hands as he talked. She could understand his nervousness, as she, too, was nervous. But she would never be able to understand that lime-green guyabera shirt!

The drive to Lake Meskwaki took them past the wildflowers that grew in profusion along fencerows and in roadside ditches. Purple bergamot, honey-colored field daisies, yellow yarrow, goldenrod, and milkweed with its pastel pink flowers, graced their view, all contributing to a wonderful floral perfume hanging over the rural blacktop. Glen's open convertible, a Saab, made the flowers especially enjoyable, a sensual delight. The long summer day carried on breezes the symphony of crickets and the cacophony of blackbirds and catbirds. Goldfinches flew in rhythmic, lilting glides from one fencepost to another, as red-tailed hawks soared, waiting for a gopher to show.

Allison thought the day was perfect.

Suddenly, a deer broke from a clump of trees near a culvert and bounded before the car. Allison saw it almost as if it were in slow motion. It seemed to her it would be easy for Glen to avoid the sleek antlered dusky-brown missile hurtling toward them. But that perception ended as the deer crashed onto the windshield, fissuring it into spider webs and splitting off fragments of glass.

Glen hit the brakes hard, bringing the car to a stop. Allison felt her seat belt tighten powerfully over her chest. She did not think she was hurt. Glen seemed OK, too.

The deer lay on the hood, stunned, a hind leg protruding a few inches over the windshield into the car, reflexively kicking, trying for traction, a hoof in motion above the radio. Blood had splattered over the hood and onto the glass. A little of it had gotten into the car and onto Allison and Glen.

Glen swore at the deer. "Get off my hood, damn deer!" he shouted.

Allison would have laughed under different circumstances. She compressed her lips forcefully to avert bursting into raucous guffaws.

The liquid amber eyes of the deer swung around, as if in answer. In them Allison discerned great pain, the eery gaze of a creature of the universe leaving this world. Her heart went out to the doomed animal.

Glen continued to curse and shout, out of control.

"Why don't you shut up?!" Allison boomed.

Glen turned to her and their eyes locked, searching each other. It was a defining moment.

Allison saw a man who could treat her like the deer, as an inconvenience to his travel, an impediment to his purposes. The chill in his eyes and the snarl in his voice scared her. Would she see and hear the same from this man if she dropped a cup of sugar in the kitchen? If she were five minutes late? If she were too tired for sex? If she had the flu and could not keep a kitchen sparkling clean?

The deer flailed hooves till it summoned up the energy and gained enough traction to escape the hood of the Saab. It struggled awkwardly off the road, disappearing into a stand of spindly willow trees. Tears sprang from Allison's eyes as the animal crashed out of sight. She could feel its suffering.

"Damn deer!" shouted Glen. "Damn you!"

Allison shot back, "Shut up. I told you to shut up!"

Silently, Glen got out of the car, walked back to the trunk, and opened it. Allison was frightened. The horrific idea seized her that he might be about to turn a gun on her.

But Glen appeared with a rag and wiped the windshield clean as best as he could. "Could you step out of the car for a second while I finish cleaning?" he asked. Allison stepped out of the Saab and stood at the roadside, watching as he put a glove on his right hand, and with that hand gathered, very methodically, the small shards of glass into a paper bag. Last, he swept up, very fastidiously, the smallest pieces with a whisk broom.

Allison observed, astounded at his volte-face from shouting, out-of-control accident victim to a seasoned soldier calmly doing his duty under siege. Once he had gotten by the initial calamity, his military background, or whatever he had, took over.

After they resumed their drive, she asked, "You're a Vietnam vet, aren't you?" She had counseled several as a social worker, and felt she knew one when she saw one.

"1967 to 1968," he answered. "Earned a medal for a firefight wound near Pleiku."

"I thought so," she put in. She plied a kleenex over the spatters of blood on her legs. She wouldn't bother with the blood on her dress till she could machine-wash it at home. "That was quite a performance. Outburst, outburst, then cool."

"Just like Vietnam," he added. "Outburst, outburst, then cool. That would be a good mantra for the whole damn worthless war."

"Can I see your medal some time?"

"If we have a second date."

"I'd like to see it on the third date, if we get there. That's long-term for me lately."

"If we kill a deer each date, it will be truly memorable," he observed coolly.

"Dates where the couple goes for road kill. Interesting. Unbelievable."

"We can sell our story to a tabloid. People will pick it up standing in grocery lines and buy the paper because of our dead deer."

* * * *

After they arrived at the Inglenook Restaurant overlooking Lake Meskwaki, they surveyed the damage to the windshield. The fractured glass would have to be replaced. It was a hazardous eyesore and the wind rushing through the spots where small shards had split off would bring in moisture when it rained.

They split up to go to the restrooms and do a thorough job washing their hands and arms and examining themselves and their clothes for deer blood. When they emerged, they both looked presentable enough for a late dinner overlooking the placid, silvered blue water of the lake.

The interior was true to the restaurant's name. In addition to traditional tables, three inglenooks along one wall offered diners seclusion and intimacy. Allison slid onto the high-backed settle on her side of the table in the inglenook they selected. Once Glen was comfortably seated, they stared deeply into each other's eyes, probing.

"That accident really got your dander up, didn't it?" he challenged.

"I don't handle deer well who jump onto my lap," she returned wryly. Actually, the deer had not upset her much. Glen had done most the upsetting with his yelling at the poor deer.

"Neither do I," Glen reacted. "That was really a very dangerous accident. We got off lucky. I hear deer sometimes come right through the windshield and people are badly hurt, even killed. We just missed that. Only a hoof and a small section of a leg made it over the windshield."

"And a little blood," added Allison.

They picked up their menus and spent a few moments studying them. Both ordered trout with baked potato, tossed salad, and burgundy wine.

There were only two other couples in the restaurant, and Glen wondered how the Inglenook made a profit. Allison opined that the profit already had been made, that they were dining late, after most the customers had come and gone.

"I'm glad we didn't order the venison," he quipped.

"We already had it," she replied in a gray monotone.

Their dinners arrived and they ate, largely in silence. Glen had expected they would talk more. He felt uncomfortable in the silence, the silence that Allison had lately come to love. He found it difficult to sustain any conversation. She resisted his efforts in that direction, reveling in the beauty of the panoramic view of Lake Meskwaki that the restaurant offered.

Glen felt stymied. After a while, he could only think of the deer blood and wait for this first and last date to end.

Allison ate her trout and mourned the deer the car had destroyed. If Glen hadn't called her **Find-A-Date** box number, she thought, the deer would still be alive.

Jess's Accident

The old woman ran the stop sign, pure and simple. She never saw it. The steeply angled, mid-morning sun made the sign invisible to her 81-year-old eyes. It was her first accident in over a half-century of driving. Ironically, she was on her way to the drivers' license examining office, only four blocks from the scene of the accident, to renew her license.

She drove a thirty-year-old Oldsmobile whose massive chrome bumper clipped the very end of a late-model Grand Prix. Her car sustained no damage, though those who later examined her bumper could see faint abrasions from the Grand Prix, which did not fare so well. It would need a new plastic rear bumper and the repair of a large dent, a job that would cost substantially.

Thelma Carson pulled over, as did the young man who drove the Grand Prix. She compulsively extracted a cigarette from a soft pack and lit up. Very nervous, frozen in place on her seat, she feared she would lose her license.

Fortunately, it was one of those rare cerulean Iowa summer days with low humidity, not even a hint of a cloud on the horizon. Jess Brownmiller unfolded himself from his Grand Prix and walked to the ancient Olds. Just my luck, he thought, to get clipped by a big car. Why couldn't it be another mid-sized car, one that wouldn't do so much one-way damage? Why couldn't he have evaded her completely?

He had seen her approaching the stop sign to his right and assumed she was slowing to a stop, but she barreled right on through. He had tried to avoid her by nudging the accelerator in the split-second he had, but she had collided with the final three inches of his car. At least this accident was not his fault, he consoled himself. His insurance rates would not go up.

Jess bent over and peered into the ancient Olds. "We collided a bit," he said, stating the obvious. "My name is Jess Brownmiller."

Thelma looked up, her wizened face taut. "I am Thelma Carson. My first accident ever," she said, her voice stressed. "I almost made it."

"Made what?"

Thelma exhaled cigarette smoke forcefully. "Made it to the drivers' license office. I was going for my renewal. Only four blocks more." She sounded glum, despondent.

She stubbed out her cigarette and pulled out another. She was so nervous, observed Jess, that she seemed unaware she had smoked little of her first cigarette. He felt for her. She looked like the compassionate, grandmotherly sort, the type that never says a mean word about anyone.

Several young boys who had been playing a pick-up soccer game in the park across the street gathered in a knot to observe Jess talking to Thelma. They had heard the loud dull thump of the collision and gathered nearby to make a soccer break of it. Jess beckoned the most mature-looking of them over to the car. He was a lanky blond kid, maybe twelve or thirteen years old, who had been coaching the younger boys.

"Could you do us a big favor?" smiled Jess.

"What is it?"

Jess pointed down the street toward a coffee shop, the Happy Doughnut, his destination before he got hit. "Could you go in there and tell them to call the police. Tell them that Jess Brownmiller needs an officer to do an accident report. Tell them to give you a dozen doughnuts, that I'll pay for them as soon as I get there."

A regular at the Happy Doughnut, they knew him well and would readily provide the young man doughnuts on hearing of the accident. Some of the morning crowd would even linger over another cup of coffee just to hear his story.

The boy seemed very pleased at the bargain. "Thank you. Good deal," he said. He smiled at his companions and took off running. Jess could hear the boys commenting to each other as to their good luck.

Jess told Thelma, "As soon as an officer does an accident report, you can go get your new license." He made a conscious effort to project a soothing tone. He knew Thelma was in shock and needed as much comfort as he could provide.

Thelma took a quick puff on her cigarette. "Good."

"That's a nice sturdy car you have there," he offered.

"My husband bought it over thirty years ago. He said it would see us both to the end. It did for him anyway. He died twenty-two years ago."

Jess was pleased that Thelma spoke several sentences. He hoped that meant she was unwinding a bit, adjusting to the reality of the accident. "You shouldn't feel too badly about this," he soothed. "You didn't intend to run that stop sign." He parted his arms expansively. "That's why these fender-benders are called accidents."

Thelma frowned, disgusted with herself, a hint of tears in her eyes. "I didn't see that stop sign. I feel so stupid." Her voice faltered. "How can I expect to get a new license when I can't see a big red stop sign staring me in the face?"

Jess smiled when she said that. Now he wanted her to say it to the officer when he arrived. He appreciated Thelma's pain. He was sympathetic. But the object of his effort was to establish in a police report that she had run the stop sign.

Where was that kid? When would a squad car arrive? He had heard that fender-benders were a low priority and suspected that something more pressing had forced the accident down the police department's list. Yet waiting would not be terribly uncomfortable. Thelma was not being at all unpleasant about the accident and she was accepting responsibility.

"You remind me of my son," noted Thelma. "Big and tall, except he's older than you."

"He lives in Quinlan?"

"No, he lives in California. He has a business out there."

"I should think that you would've moved out there to be near him and enjoy the mild winters."

159

"I tried that right after my husband died, but I didn't like it. I came back to Quinlan after a year. I didn't like all the traffic and weird people in California. I like it more back here in Iowa."

"Your son must miss you a lot."

Thelma gave a dismissive wave of her hand. "He doesn't miss me. If he did, I'd still be out there in California. I didn't realize how he had grown so apart from me until I went out there to live. It just didn't work out."

"You didn't like living with him and his family?"

"I didn't like living in the same town with him. I had my own place. I didn't like them stopping by any time they wished, like I was some sort of convenience stop."

Jess thought that his own mother would love that situation if she got as old as Thelma. She appreciated her sons dropping by to see her and Dad now. She would love it even more in advanced old age. He wondered what went wrong in the relationship between Thelma and her son. "So they visit you here every year?" he asked.

Thelma shook her head. "It has been two years since the last visit. I like it that way. I keep in touch by phone and letters. A visit is a hassle. I don't want much company. For me, the good life is getting in my car and going downtown for a coffee break." Thelma's voice broke when she said the word **car.** Losing her license because of the accident would mean losing the independence she treasured.

Abruptly, Jess's attention was diverted to a noise in the park. The big blond kid had returned with the doughnuts and was distributing them among the boisterous younger boys. Above the din, the big kid shouted at Jess, "They called the police. They'll get here as soon as they can." He paused, searching for words. "They have a burglary or something to take care of."

"What did he say?" asked Thelma, straining to hear.

"He said the police are busy with more serious matters and won't be here for a while."

"How long's a while?"

Jess shrugged. "I wish I knew. But we can't stay out here much longer. You're too old for this kind of abuse."

Thelma nodded and took a long pull on her cigarette. She was no longer so nervous. She sat quietly.

Jess thought of his own mother, now in her late forties, and how he would not want her to wait an indeterminate time for a police car, especially if she got to be Thelma's age. The rational part of him wanted to make sure her insurance paid for the damage to his new Grand Prix. But he could not be so coldly calculating. She was too fragile and vulnerable to wait on the street any longer.

"You can go now," he told her. "I'll take care of everything." He did not even exchange addresses and the names of insurance companies. Entangling her in the coils and toils of even a minor accident claim seemed inappropriate now.

Thelma thanked him, but did not do so profusely. She wasted no time at all in driving off toward the drivers' license examining office.

Jess walked to his Grand Prix. He felt grandly lifted that he had freed Thelma from any responsibility for the accident. He would pay for his repairs out of pocket and not even notify his insurance agent. Just call it early Mother's Day for someone else's mother, he thought, justifying himself to himself.

*   *   *   *

The usual crowd at the Happy Doughnut looked at him expectantly as he entered the coffee shop. They wanted to hear about the dent in his car, how it happened, the whole story. Most of them were retired. The details of a fender-bender would bridge the ennui of their day.

Jess told them that an old lady had hit him and that he had let her go. As he spoke, a Quinlan P. D. squad car made a left turn in view of the coffee shop. Everyone locked out the window to watch it travel toward an accident that no longer existed.

161

G. Louis Heath, Ph. D.

Ed, one of the Happy Doughnut regulars, observed, "That cop will be pleased. One less report to write."

But Jess was thinking that not all accidents require a report, that some are more like experiences that verge on epiphanies. The dent had become a window on the life of an elderly widow living in a very different dimension than his own. He would never again think of anyone that old in the same way.

Jess sipped his freshly brewed late-morning coffee and spread out the house newspaper. He read the headlines but they did not register. He could only think of Thelma Carson. The only thing that bothered him was that she never told him where she took her coffee breaks. He wondered why that bothered him as he bit into his doughnut.

Our Soldier

(Planet UE-122, April 12, 2843) – Three million light years from the sun, intergalactic political tensions have come to a head in the form of a global war on the giant planet UE-122, a war which began April sixth. Both forces, ours and theirs, have been quickly, vastly reduced to pathetic remnants of what they began with, owing to the enemy's unrestricted use of state-of-the-art laser and nuclear weaponry in defiance of the principles of the Geneva Convention.

It is, to say the least, a dirty, hot war, with excruciating temperatures, and to make matters particularly aggravating, the silicate-like crust of barren UE-122 flakes off and sticks painfully to our soldier, Light Laser Specialist M-2-2000 (whose name I cannot report due to security measures the military has imposed on the press), making him a thoroughly miserable combatant, and proving once again that "war is hell" and should be avoided in the future, at least if no longer profitable. Light Laser Specialist M-2-2000 is only one of millions of our soldiers on UE-122, but his story is typical, except for the fact that he is the only one still alive to continue the fighting.

Our soldier looks forward to finishing his tour of duty on UE-122. The enemy has fought such a dirty, unprincipled war, using their biggest nukes and lasers, even if it has meant killing more of their own soldiers than ours. Our soldier can find nothing to recommend this war!

Our soldier has told this correspondent that he signed on for duty on UE-122 in the hope he might test his finely honed individual combat skills against individual enemy soldiers. If he could have done that, rather than watch, as spectator-survivor, 500 million on each side die the most hellacious, painful deaths possible anywhere in the galaxies, then The Ultimate War, fought to settle who will control the galaxies for millions of light years around, would have held some chivalrous attraction for

163

him personally. But the aliens, with their scrofulous, weird, horrific looks and their weapons that make H-bombs look like toys, have had nothing to do with fair, manly combat. Accordingly and ironically, the death and destruction have become so widespread and total that The Ultimate War has come down to our soldier, our only survivor, combatting the final survivor of their military, their soldier. Our soldier against their soldier. One on one. Very chivalrous, very sporting.

Our soldier would like to blast their soldier clean off UE-122. That would teach it a lesson and perhaps give our side The Final Victory and enable M-2-2000 to take a chunk of alien home as a souvenir.

Today our soldier saw something moving in the nuclear haze on the gray murky horizon. It looked like the grotesque alien scuttering along a ridge. "That ugly top part of the alien," our soldier muttered, "would be worth zapping if only to beautify the (expletive deleted) view!"

Our soldier crouched and carefully aimed his laser at the alien and fired. Immediately the alien fell upon its grotesque appendages. A direct hit! Light Laser Specialist M-2-2000 was elated, moving quickly to the alien, which was fast dying of its wound. Jupiter! It was so very nauseating to watch the horrid creature die. Our soldier could hardly bear to gaze upon the beast, convulsing desperately, a freak of nature, with absolutely no scales, horns, or protective slime. It had only two arms and two legs, and most repulsive of all, was that ghastly white skin.

Simmel's Triad

"What a long eighteen years it's been!" thought Larry Smithson as he helped his eighteen-year-old son John pack the family van. He carried a large box of CDs and books. They were near the end of loading, and perspiration had beaded his forehead. He pulled out his handkerchief and wiped his brow. "Almost done," he sighed.

He and Sybil were very proud. Their only child would soon be off to college, a milestone they were pleased to reach. It hardly seemed possible that they and John had made it. Nothing like this seemed possible when they started with a seven-pound-four-ounce bundle of flesh. Making it to high school graduation and getting accepted at prestigious Odin College in Quinlan, Iowa confirmed that the eighteen-year journey of youth, fraught with peril, had been traveled successfully.

Others in Tracy, Wisconsin had not been so successful. Those people's children offered one kind of measure for John. It was a negative measure, but an effective one. One acquaintance's son had committed suicide. Another had been busted for drug dealing. Yet another's daughter had been killed in a car crash. As Larry occasionally said, "We'll settle for non-tragedy for John. Anything beyond that is a blessing." And Sybil usually added, "We love him and wish him the best. Just so he's healthy and happy. That's what we want for him."

It was early morning, and Larry, Sybil, and John were finishing packing the van for the trip to Odin College, to take John to begin his freshman year. They busied themselves carrying boxes, suitcases, garment bags, a goose-neck lamp, and sundry sports equipment from the house. They carefully fitted all the stuff into the van.

A variety of warblers, the first of those to move south for the season, were bobbing amid the heather and lilac bushes surrounding their split-level home, situated on a wooded five acres. Larry, a birdwatcher, eyed the warblers enviously. They rarely lived more than five years, and they all reproduced well before their allotted years were up.

Here he was escorting his "little warbler" to college, just after celebrating his eighteenth birthday. It was a long haul from "conception to commencement," he reflected. He almost burst out laughing. He found the phrase amusing.

John, at eighteen, represented maybe four generations of warblers. Was that meaningful or what? Biologically determined as they were, limited to a few trills for communication, the issue of genealogy did not exist for them. They were but part of the eternal flow of warbler life. With homo sapiens, each person was different. Each had a distinct history. There was individuation, and that had brought Larry one helluva lot of long-term responsibility.

John was in a grumpy mood that afternoon as he got ready for the drive to Odin. He wanted to go to college, to finally leave home, but it was difficult. He had tried to make it easier by living in the basement rec room for the summer, as a sort of halfway point between home and college. Living down there had proved a burden. Three months of it had made him irritable.

Larry could read the scene better than Sybil, who had, he thought, done much more of the spoiling of John than he had. He thought it was too late to unspoil an eighteen-year-old who had been catered to all his life. Yet the spoiling had not caused tragedy, at least not yet. Though he had a lot of regrets, he felt he had done his best to counteract an overindulgent mother, and that he had achieved modest success. His son was a viable young man despite his flaws, a young man capable of building a life that at least would carry its load, and maybe even contribute a little to society.

Larry took substantial pride in the fact that his son would soon matriculate at one of the best liberal arts colleges in the Midwest. And that isn't bad, he thought, a hint of a smile appearing on his lips.

Larry drove the van over the gravel access road from their home onto the county road that led to the state highway. He drove past fields of corn and ginseng. In the backseat, John rolled his window down and rested his arm on the frame. Larry did not say anything. He left that to Sybil. He knew she would soon register her disapproval over the danger.

"It's dangerous to put your elbow out like that," warned Sybil. "A semi might take it off for you."

John retracted his arm into the car, his face sullen. "Thanks for telling me, Mom," he said in a saturnine voice. Sybil who sat on the passenger side up front, glanced back at John. "Thank you, John. That makes us feel better." She looked to Larry who nodded.

The traffic was, as usual, sparse on the county road. An old, green car approached from the opposite direction and John waved. The green car honked.

"Who was that?" asked Sybil.

"Ronny Miller," returned John.

"Is he going to college?"

"Too stupid."

"Too stupid?" Sybil furrowed her brow. "You shouldn't talk about your classmates that way."

"He's not my classmate. He's my ex-classmate. He's a nerd, a burnout, a loser."

"You shouldn't talk about anyone that way," said Sybil. "Remember, I'm your mother. You could use a little of my advice."

"He's still stupid!"

Larry had a good inner laugh. Here they were on the way to depositing John at Odin College and she was showing a rare glimmer of discipline. It was too late for that. Eighteen years too late.

Recently, he had been re-reading his old college sociology text. He had become absorbed in the chapter on the work of the German sociologist George Simmel, who had written on "social triads." Whenever someone joins a pair or "dyad," someone in the newly created triad benefits. Simmel had termed the phenomenon, "the third one who benefits," which, in German, was but one long word.

The sociology of two was very different from the sociology of three in Simmel's world. The dynamics were a whole different social ball game. Larry wanted to learn to play that game.

What Larry was doing was what his old sociology prof had termed "applied sociology." It would be great to avoid the fray, to distance himself and benefit from conflict. It was a difficult triangulation to achieve, but he planned to do it as often as he could. This was his "Odin resolution," the new leaf he was turning as he turned John over to Odin.

Larry, Sybil, and John drove a couple hours until it was pit-stop time. Larry took an exit that looked promising.

The poplar and box elder trees twinkled their leaves in a soft breeze as the sun illuminated them. The trees were gorgeous, piercingly refulgent, gleaming as if they were about to ignite. Where sun reflected off leaf, that, thought Larry, was about the most beautiful feature of nature.

"What's that?" asked Sybil, pointing at some buildings in the near distance.

"A big pit stop," speculated John.

"Let's drive to that," suggested Sybil.

Larry nodded and nudged the accelerator. Was it their pit stop? He hoped so. He easily found a parking spot in the half-full lot. They were at "Adventureland," the large gold-on-green sign atop the main building proclaimed.

"Let's go in," enthused Sybil.

"OK with me," concurred John.

Larry nodded.

They got out and walked toward the entrance. As they neared it, a plump, middle-aged couple approached, smiling.

"We have tickets," the woman in floral-pattern summerweight dress said. "Do you want them?"

"For rides?" asked Sybil.

"Yes, for rides."

"Wow, great," enthused John.

"Thank you," said Larry, taking them off her extended palm. He wondered what a corpulent couple with no children in tow were doing going on rides. Perhaps they had gone on none, once they had trembled at the gates of Tilt-A-Whirl. He knew that ride. It made him nauseous just to think about.

Larry wanted to say he thought they were looking for a pit stop, not a hair-raising carnival ride. But he caught himself, taking refuge in the confines of Simmel's Triad.

After they had pit-stopped, they explored Adventureland. Garish snack stands and raucous game concessions abounded, all in blazing, glossy colors. The smell of funnel cakes, corn dogs, chili dogs, cheese nachos and other fattening carny fare drifted on a soft breeze.

They stopped at a stand where John got a funnel cake, Sybil a corn dog, and Larry an orange drink.

The day was gorgeous. A few clouds cruised overhead across a baby-blue sky. A gentle breeze ruffled the lofty row of red, green, and yellow Adventureland flags. Larry breathed in deeply. It felt good. He felt free. The day was pristine and John was leaving home. That meant freedom. Enjoy, he thought. Enjoy it fully. It has been a long time coming, this, my big reward.

They continued up the midway toward the rides as John nibbled his funnel cake and Sybil worked on her corn dog.

"Yours looks good," said Sybil.

John took a bite. "Tastes good, too."

"Remember, dear, it's junk food," she said. "Don't eat too much of it at Odin College. Remember, you're laying the foundation now for good health in your middle age and beyond."

"Yeah."

Larry nodded, smiling. A hundred yards up the midway, John's funnel cake looked increasingly delicious, and he decided to have one himself to accompany his orange drink. He spotted a bright yellow-and-red kiosk emblazoned with gold starbursts. A very heavyset woman with several bracelets on each arm sat in the kiosk, waiting for her next customer. He wondered how she could prepare and serve food with bracelets clattering.

He ordered a funnel cake. He had never had one before.

John ordered a lemon drink to wash the remnants of the sugary funnel cake off his teeth. Larry paid the woman and they continued toward the Tilt-A-Whirl that loomed at the end of the midway.

As Larry nibbled his funnel cake, John pointed to it. "That's good, Dad. I enjoyed mine."

"Tastes good," Larry agreed. "I've never had one before."

"Oh, look," burbled Sybil. "There's a petting zoo. Isn't that baby goat cute?"

The redolence of animals mixed with the flavor of Larry's funnel cake as they stopped to view children amid goats, guinea hens, sheep, a pony, and ducks and geese. One parent had accompanied his daughter among the animals. He wore earphones, listening to a small radio clipped to his belt. His little girl petted the animals, largely oblivious of him. He had tuned into the radio. She had tuned him out.

"Where's that cute goat?" asked John.

"Over there by that little girl," pointed out Sybil.

Over there by the man listening to the radio, thought Larry. The thin, young man looked very absorbed in his radio. With earphones looped over his head, he reminded Larry of some kind of electronic technician. The wires stemming from the earphones, converging beneath his chin, seemed to frame an oddly abstract beard for the man who had no facial hair.

The man with the radio glanced at Larry, Sybil, and John. He knew he was being observed. His face turned sour, and he abruptly left the enclosure surrounding the animals, stopping just outside the iron-pipe fence. He focussed his eyes on his daughter, blocking out Larry, Sybil, and John. The little girl continued to pet the baby goat, unfazed by her Dad's departure.

When "Dad" walked away, disappearing on the midway, the three of them wondered just who he was. Maybe he was a total stranger to the girl.

They watched the girl pet the goat a while longer and left. If she was there alone much longer, someone might need to report the strange situation.

*   *   *   *

When Larry saw the Tilt-A-Whirl gyrating crazily, he became disgusted at the idea of riding it. 'You go ahead," he told Sybil and John. He pulled out his wallet and gave them the tickets the couple had given them. "I'll stay down here and watch." He paused, glancing at the top of the so-called amusement ride. "Enjoy," he added, his voice tinged with sarcasm so subtle he was sure he had not disrupted Simmel's triad.

The Tilt-A-Whirl came to a stop, and Larry watched his wife and son board. He noted how they were enjoying themselves. This made him happy. He finished the last of his funnel cake as the Tilt-A-Whirl swung into frenetic, mind-blowing motion.

As he watched the thrill ride rotate and gyrate, Larry thought of the little girl in the petting zoo and whether she needed help. Who was that man? Who was she?

When John and Sybil disembarked the Tilt-A-Whirl, they complained of nausea. They wanted to find a place to sit down before they got on the road again. They wanted to give their stomachs an opportunity to settle.

They sat on a bright red bench a few yards off the midway. Sybil and John commiserated with each other about their upset stomachs. After a few minutes, as the early afternoon sun beat down, Sybil rose. "I feel a lot better. How about you, John?"

"I'm about back to normal," he said.

All the way to Quinlan, about all they talked about was the little girl in the petting zoo. They created several possible stories to explain what they saw. Or, at least John and Sybil did.

Larry mostly nodded and smiled, all the way to Odin College.

Happy Workers

Everyone at Glover Electric had identical schedules. They arrived, lunch in hand, at eight o'clock in the morning. They left at five in the evening. When the torrid summer days arrived, they shifted to a seven a.m. start, going off-duty at 3:30. Eighty-two employees, season after season, year after year, followed the same schedule, doing much the same things.

Celia and Diane were two of the eighty-two who had put their work lives into a finely honed groove. They were now in their twenty-second and twenty-third years respectively at the factory.

Celia was married to Phil and they had two grown boys. One son, Burt, had graduated from college and had a good job. The other, Gabe, would soon start his senior year at a nearby private liberal arts college, highly regarded Odin College, in Quinlan, Iowa.

Diane was married to Frank. They had recently become grandparents. Their eldest daughter, Sonia, had given them a granddaughter, Amanda, and they were thrilled. They had stuck a bumper sticker on their car proclaiming their new joyous status.

Celia and Diane rode together to work daily, either in Celia's Pontiac or Diane's Chevy. Just as much as anyone in their immediate families, they had come to know each other well. They conversed during the half-hour commute to and from work. They continued their conversation at their work stations, which stood side by side.

They were best friends. They relied on each other inside and outside the workplace. They often engaged in lengthy phone conversations in the evening, although they knew they would see each other early the next morning. They had forged a steel-like bond.

173

On their drive, one May morning, Celia and Diane discussed losing weight. They often lost weight with the latest fad diet, only to eventually fall off the wagon and gradually regain the weight, often plus some. So, it was predictable that the topic would come up for the umpteenth time.

"I've gotta lose some weight!" exclaimed Diane. "Or else I will have to buy all new clothes," she added in a tone of dismay.

"There goes your 401(k), on its very own diet," Jested Celia, a bit elliptically.

"What's the use of having a retirement account if your fat body falls dead before you retire," returned Diane as she wheeled her Chevy around a sharp curve in the road.

The recently greened trees and newly blossomed flowers gave a beauty and scent that had been sorely missed during the winter. Diane felt vaguely that it was the return of leaf and flower that had prompted her to consider returning to a diet. That is maybe why her diets failed. They were seasonal things (though not every season). Her body wanted to slough off fat the way deciduous trees threw off winter and became green again.

"That's an excellent point," agreed Celia. "We better give the diet another try. After all, we're getting up there in years and could die if we don't take care of ourselves." She paused to roll down the passenger-side window an inch. "A little fresh air won't hurt."

So went their stylized diet conversation, ebullient banter. They had repeated it many times before as prelude to yet another diet attempt.

Diane and Celia knew each other well, like they knew their work on the assembly line. Year-in and year-out, installing the same gizmo in the same widget, again, again, and again, to virtual infinity. They each assembled the same panel for transformers that would be installed all over Iowa. They knew each other that way, intimately, like they knew the transformer components they assembled.

Within their circles of work and private life, Celia and Diane considered themselves happy. They were happy that spring. Diane had a granddaughter that brought joy to her life and Celia was absorbed in the lives of her sons. Their local union had won a substantial wage increase for them, avoiding the strike that had been threatened. Their husbands were healthy, though a bit flabby. Things were going well.

In July, on a humid, sizzling day, close to a record high, Celia was driving. She had the air conditioner on full blast, and she said in a louder-than-usual voice, 'How is Frank doing?" She often asked this question in their stylized conversations, just as Diane asked her, "How is Phil doing these days?" They were questions like "How are you?," part of a protocol rather than a form of communication, intended to bridge the ennui of a drive rather than establish profoundly human contact.

Diane made a perfunctory swipe at the dust on the dash. "Oh, he is just fine. Loves his job."

"Phil loves his job too," put in Celia. "He'll love that job till the day he retires."

This launched a few minutes of small talk about "my Frank" and "my Phil," zesty gab, full of laughs and one-liners.

Over the summer, through the fall, into winter, they talked about things—thing-things, event-things, and people-things, the things that filled their lives. Cars, boats, pizzas, restaurants, cigarettes, cameras. Husbands and children and a grandchild who made them happy. Commencements, parties, diets, and church services that made them happy. These were all things that made them happy, like the tools they used in the factory made them happy.

175

G. Louis Heath, Ph. D.

A Form Of Clinging

Paul Leslie was returning to his hometown for his sixty-year class reunion. As he walked the main street in the little downtown, he could hardly believe six decades had passed since his graduation from Plumas High School. But it was very true. The downtown he'd known intimately as a youngster was sixty years older and it had changed a good deal, but it was still Plumas, California, the town of 8,000 where he'd grown up. He was now 78, and he figured he'd better get back for the sixty-year reunion of his high school graduating class, to see Plumas and his few surviving school buddies once more, before he ran out of time to do so.

Since his wife Barbara had died two years ago, reunions were not nearly as important to him. He'd thought that he'd savor the old-school tie even more. But Barb was more his link to his classmates than he had previously realized. Even though she was not one of them, she was the one who enabled him to connect with his classmates. She wrote the letters and made the phone calls. Without her, the connections ended.

Now, he mostly wanted to be alone in the town of his youth, at the base of Ishi Mountain, with the Little Salmon River running through it.

Every walk he took made the memories flow. The pastel yellow stucco apartments just off the main street still stood, but the pair of persimmon trees that flanked them were gone. He remembered with a rush the wonderful taste of the persimmons from the trees that stood there during his youth. In late September and early October, the heart-shaped fruits would turn from green to bright orange, fully ripe. For three or four years, Paul had observed the tragedy of overripe persimmons falling to the ground and rotting before he finally screwed up the courage to ask permission to pick the glossy orange fruits on shares. The owner had enthusiastically consented.

Walking the downtown square was an exercise that Marcel Proust, the French author who specialized in memories, would have approved. The smell of the July air off the nearby river evoked his fishing adventures as a youngster. He bicycled from his home on Robinson Street four blocks to the river, where he waded into the riffles and cast his spinner. The smell of the river and the feel of it pushing against his legs came back to him on his walk, powerful memories that took his mind back six decades and more.

As a kid, he had caught salmon that he classified as "monsters," but hardly ever exceeded ten pounds. The remarkable battles they put up, and—if he were lucky enough to land them—their beautiful sheen and sharp, rebuking eyes, still haunted him. The sense of being connected to a river that yielded sizeable salmon, and being able to safely bicycle to it and fish into the darkness, seemed, in retrospect, a high privilege.

His hometown owed much of its history, its collective memory, to the river. A fact of people, it derived from a fact of nature, the eternal water from the Sierras that gave birth to Plumas. Local boosters and patrons of bars liked to claim that the founders of the town had conquered nature, digging gold out of the earth and sluicing and panning it from the river. But it would have been more appropriate to say that, in the cosmic order of nature and her forces, that they had scratched a living for a while as the eternal river and the mountains looming above them looked on stoically. The gold had petered out and most the people had left, leaving a very small town behind. In the end, the river and the mountains had continued in bigness, witnesses to the passing scene of a small gold fever.

Paul's view was unusually geological and timeless. His classmates thought more in terms of the clothing styles, car models, and fads of their generation. He was different. That is why, for his sixty-year reunion, he was coming home as much, if not more so, to the town and its natural surroundings, as he was to the reunion banquet in the Sierra Restaurant.

Only forty-one of the graduating class of 132 survived. As the group thinned, each graduate's relationship to it had become more intense and significant. A survivor mentality had come to accent the reunions. It had started a couple reunions ago and had become intensely palpable. Paul saw it as a positive thing, the last of a generation clinging to each other. But he dreaded this phenomenon should he be one of the last ten survivors. He wasn't so sure he would want to join the nine others in a reunion, even if they pressured him. That would be a much too powerful form of clinging for him.

Paul arrived among the first at the Sierra Restaurant. He pulled into the parking lot just behind Susan Gerber and her husband Ralph. Susan smiled and Ralph waved. The blacktop gave off heat with an asphalt smell, at five in the evening, that stifled them. They stood near some of the palm trees and oleanders that had been part of the backdrop of their youth, and, farther, in the distance, digger pines on low mountains. The nearest mountains showed deep cuts of red laterite that had been created by early hydraulic placer mining, followed by over a century of erosion. They drank it in nostalgically, for it was home, scars and all. Then, together, they entered the restaurant that offered cool relief from the blistering heat.

Ralph got drinks for the three of them as they waited for their classmates to arrive. They sat at a window with a view of the Sierra foothills. Just before them stood a fountain whose waters a slight breeze rippled. Soon, they got onto the topic of those who had died since the last reunion. It always happened that way. Each reunion became, in part, a memorial event for those deceased during the previous five years.

"D'ya hear that Mike Snyder died?" asked Ralph.

"News to me," replied Paul. "It must have been recent."

"No, three years ago," put in Susan.

Paul's jaw tightened. "I've been sort of out of touch since Barb died."

Ralph and Susan had not heard that Barb had died, which surprised Paul. But, how were they to know, unless he told them or someone they knew? Over two thousand miles away, living in Quinlan, Iowa and teaching at Odin College, without a grapevine, news would not travel at all. He felt guilty that he hadn't done his duty to notify someone in Plumas to get the word out. He just sort of assumed Barb would take care of the networking, even in death, which comprised an interesting psychological twist on his part. He had yet to acknowledge fully that the life that his late wife had kept intact for them for fifty-two years no longer existed. He needed to begin taking responsibility for himself.

Paul told his friends about Barb's stroke and how she had become incapacitated by slurred speech and walking problems. After eighteen months, she had another massive stroke and died.

Ralph and Susan tried to follow with something upbeat. They had taken a winter vacation in Mazatlan. They had been told that was the spot for the retired, more so by far than Hawaii, which had grown too artificial, expensive, and condo-ridden. Mazatlan still offered a slice of authentic Mexico, along with the touristy, commercial Mexico, and it was a true bargain compared to Hawaii.

Susan spoke of the paragliding, the children pestering them with souvenirs for sale, and the excellent meals they had eaten at the hotel. But then her face tensed, her eyes dimmed, and she said darkly, "Sometimes you get even more than you bargained for."

Ralph made a don't-tell face, but Susan had piqued Paul's interest. His eyes asked for the story. Susan gave a nervous smile and began. She could kick herself. Throughout high school to this very moment, she talked too much. Everyone regarded it as an ebullient part of her personality, except Ralph, who viewed it as an incurable disease.

"Oh, it's not much really," said Susan, "but I'm going to tell you about it. It's sort of an interesting story."

Paul took a slow pull on his beer and nodded.

"Well, Ralph got really sick down there—the water probably. It put him flat on his back, and I got really worried. He didn't want to get up at all. He was kind of paralyzed he said, and not getting better."

Ralph nodded. He never was much of a talker. Paul knew he would only contribute a few words, if at all.

"So, what did you do?" asked Paul.

"I didn't know what to do. He was running a high temperature. I could tell that by feeling his forehead. His whole body ached, he said." Ralph nodded again, his face its usual blank. "I got really desperate, so I called the front desk at our hotel. They called an ambulance."

"Things got interesting then," put in Ralph laconically, his face remaining expressionless.

"How interesting?" Paul prodded.

Susan took a gulp from the pink drink she had ordered from the cash bar. (She only drank pink drinks.) "Well, the ambulance came and a couple of medics came to our room. They were both young guys. One took Ralph's pulse and temperature and checked him out. They consulted each other in Spanish, too fast for us to understand, then told us they must get him"—she extended her arm toward her husband—"to the hospital fast. Might be serious they said."

Ralph gave another nod, like a metronome, deadpan.

"They put him on a gurney and cinched him in. Carried him down to the ambulance and drove off." Susan halted, holding back words.

The story absorbed Paul. "And?" he nudged.

"It took me four days to get him back. It was awful what we went through down there. I hope you never have to go through something like that!"

*   *   *   *

The gist of the horror story was that Ralph got well in a little over a day, but the hospital would not release him until Susan paid in full. Since she had maxed out their credit cards and had little cash remaining in dollars, she could not pay. And each day the bill increased substantially.

Ralph regarded himself a hostage and tried to escape one night, but security caught him. They strapped him to his bed to prevent further such misadventures. Only when Ralph begged and screamed, would they even allow him to visit the bathroom. They stopped feeding him regularly, but they continued to bill him at the regular rate, even adding some for the extra security he required.

Susan visited the U.S. consulate and they began to look into the matter. Not wanting to depend solely on them, she continued on her own hook, getting a favorite uncle to wire her a substantial sum of money. When she went to the hospital, they gave her a hard time about the bill, saying it would take some more time to compute, or something like that. They went out of their way, it seemed to her, to speak entirely in Spanish.

She took up an unobtrusive vigil in a little park by the hospital, observing quietly. She sat on a bench as she waited for someone in a green uniform to exit. Ralph had told her in his last phone call that the security personnel wore green.

After a lengthy wait, she saw a man wearing green leave the hospital. She approached him and managed to communicate that she was the wife of Ralph. The man spoke very little English, but she felt she had succeeded in arranging a deal to spring Ralph. She handed the man a newspaper containing her money. He smiled oleaginously, bowing as he backed away. He left her in the little park and disappeared down a palm-lined avenue.

She never saw the man or her money again. She should have let the American consulate's staff handle the problem. They got Ralph out on the evening of the fourth day, paying the bill. Susan and Ralph reimbursed the consulate after they returned home.

Paul's mind wrapped around the story in an intensely prehensile way. He savored it. It had somehow provoked an epiphany within him. For the first time, he felt he didn't need Barb any more. He looked forward to the next story that this reunion would produce. Suddenly, he had begun to enjoy the single life, as a person who felt complete though shorn of his distaff half.

The breeze from the mountains picked up, rustling the delicate mimosa trees and loud-red-flowered bottle-brush bushes. The water in the fountain in front of the restaurant rippled as if possessed by water spirits. A few wooly clouds had appeared over the mountains.

The fall salmon migration would soon begin and the persimmons would ripen and become delicious as the fish battled their eternal way upriver. It was all a form of clinging that Paul relished.

"Mountie Prof" And Ten Other Story-Poems

"Mountie Prof"

Sometimes they called me "Doc."
Mostly they called me "Dr. Heath."
But now my students address
me, "Mountie Prof." I smile.
At Mount St. Clare College,
that means you've arrived, that
you're established. It took me
twenty years to achieve that cachet
of distinction here, to reach that
level of acceptance, to win that honor.
Others have done so far more quickly
but none with more joy.

On this bluff overlooking the
Mississippi River, in this quiet
Iowa river town, we "Mountie
Profs" have transformed lives,
including our own. We have
taught youth from farms and
small towns to appreciate
different cultures and we have
helped our international students
to appreciate Iowa. We have
taught them all the content of
our disciplines, and some have
even caught the contagion of
our passion for the knowledge
we dispense. Occasionally, one
goes on to eclipse our level of

knowledge and passion,
and we are pleasurably awed at
what we have wrought.

For that we truly deserve the honorific
title,
    "Mountie Prof."

Thrusting The Sudden Series

of painful memories aside, Chuck went outside
to split wood. Wood comprised the pith of his
antidote to pain. If only he had a defense that

could strike down the demons before they latched
on. He swung his maul, stroking the wedge
deeper and deeper into the oak, until it split.

He looked up sweatily from time to time to check
the ascent of the sun behind the windbreak of
poplar and osage orange. These sun checks and
the glistening patina on his face settled him. It
had been years since his wife had been nibbled to
death by cancer that put her down so agonizingly
slowly. He tended to her every need with ceaseless
love, dreading the losing of her, the center of his
universe. The end finally came, and as her hand
slipped from his—as he finally let go at the
doctor's urging—he knew he would never be the
same.

Splitting logs, driving the wedge into each
oak log, the ringing of the metal thumping into
the wood conveyed his mind momentarily beyond
his mourning for Lucille, a mourning that had been
acute over five years, the pain only remitting—or
so it seemed—when he stroked oak. When the pain
would diminish, even his therapist could not, by now,
advise. Perhaps he had loved too much.

The sun had cleared the highest poplars and shone
full on him. He gave a short smile and swung again.

G. Louis Heath, Ph. D.

Perhaps It Made Him Uncomfortable

the way the woman asked him
about the pack of cigarettes
he had in his hand,
like maybe he was trying
to hide them or something.

So he paid her perfunctorily,
containing his ire. Once
outside Jolly Market, he
opened his Marlboros,
pulled out a smoke,
and lit up.

That woman clerk, the environ-
mentalists, and the cancer alarm-
ists could go to hell.

He exhaled. Defiance felt good.
The smoke filled his nostrils and
emerged as two jet contrails,
or so he imagined,
never to meet again, a measure
of tar and nicotine and the mis-
measure of him.

The un-jet speed of a cowboy
who drove a '92 Toyota pickup
along the vista of a flaming orange
vista flicked with gray ash
enabled him to pull out the ash tray
and laugh at his own cremation.

186

I Listened Hard

but I can't remember the specifics
of what was said at the meeting
with my lawyer.

I can't even remember the gist of
what he told me. At $100 an hour
I should have taken notes. But what
he had to say was so very hard on
me, my pen stayed still in my hand.

I have pushed it all into vagueness,
though, of course, I recall the topic.

At $100 an hour, it was important.
It was also painful.

I refuse to discuss it.

G. Louis Heath, Ph. D.

Harvey, November 23, 2000

I read in the paper this morning
about a guy in a county home
in southwestern Iowa whose
family has just found him after
67 years.

Harvey's been in the Taylor County
Home since he was ten. (They used
to call it the "poor farm.") He talks
to himself a lot, mimicking voices.
(He's real good at that.) But he does
not have multiple personality disorder.

The article says he's retarded and has
never held a job or married. No one
in his family had seen him since he
was ten. Some knew his father had
had a son but they weren't sure about
anything specific, except that the son
was most certainly deceased.

Finally, a determined genealogist among
them found him. They've even decor-
ated his room with family photos and
brought in a new armchair to enhance
life in his austere room.

The photo of Harvey on the front page
of the **Des Moines Register** shows him
holding a framed picture of his father.
When they gave it to him, he said,
"It's my Dad," immediately,

after all these years.

The paper this morning tugged at my heart.

It's Thanksgiving today.

G. Louis Heath, Ph. D.

The Trucker

was wearing slightly washed-out,
oil-stained jeans and a grimy T-shirt
that read, "I'M HAVING A BAD DAY."
When he sat dcwn beside me at the
counter in the I-80 truck stop near
Davenport, Iowa, I felt my spine tense up.

I was surprised when he pulled out
his correspondence course from some
University—it began with an S—and
started to work, on Philosophy. This
took me aback because he was a grimy
                    trucker.

Maybe, I thought, if truckers don't do
Philosophy, neither our trucks nor our
theories will run smoothly on our high-
ways, nor will they be able to negotiate
the ruts and bumps of the byways.

I could see he was studying Wittgenstein's
Blue Book. I got excited. Ludwig was
part of the Vienna Circle! He was close to
                    the great Carnap!

I have never though of truckers the same
                    since.

His Name Won't Ring

many bells outside the legal profession
      they said.
But as the head of Iowa's judiciary, he
has been one of the most powerful
people in state government.

The relative anonymity of a Supreme
Court justice does not ring bells. It
pulls levers.

I like that.

Give me a lever
over a bell
anytime.

Gravitas over
a tinkle
any anytime.

G. Louis Heath, Ph. D.

Shopping For A Couch

My wife shifts her weight onto
                    her right foot.
I'm thinking how I've never
personally bought a piece of
furniture in my whole life.
I'm thinking that if she wants me
to seriously consider this couch,
I'll need to rack out on it, and
see if my feet hang over the edge.

I'm thinking how we're just one day
short of our seventh anniversary.
Jill eyes me intently. "So," she says.
She and the saleswoman look at me,
        but in different ways. Or at least
        I think so. I hope so anyway.

I ask, "What exactly is the difference
between a couch and a sofa?"

Or a rock and a pebble, or a fragrance
and a perfume, or even a compact
and a mid-size, widget or car, you
                    name it.

It Is Not Like The Chief

of the Meskwaki to let the sun go down
on the matter like this. Then Iron Shirt says,
The first step was to steal as many horses
as we could. But he saw his mother get mad,
Iowa Indian mad, and he spoke no more of the
pilfered ponies. And the sun went down on
           the matter.

On the white side, Jed said, My father not
only escaped the Indians, he escaped the
wolves. Which sounds like this movie is
portraying whites as genetically superior.

But fifteen minutes later, Jed said, For the
first time I saw these Indians as I never
saw them before. Suddenly, they were people
who laughed and dreamed. (The fifteen
minutes represented three years in real time,
so you can see Jed had plenty enough time
for an attitude adjustment.)

The Chief's sons were born and they all pleased
his eyes. They all were killed by war. He longed
to see his granddaughter before his eyes were
           closed to the sky.

That was many beaver skins ago.

G. Louis Heath, Ph. D.

A Thump And A Crash

of glass reverberated into my living room,
rousing me from my spine on my La-Z-Boy.
The **Herald** would have to wait. There was
an accident at the corner of Bluff and North.

The crumpled fenders had engaged each other
like mechanical beasts in a fight to the death.
The whole sorry scene reminded me of a kiss
on a bad blind date where random lips collide,
locked in a deathly grip of lips, or so it seemed
to me.

In point of fact, the drivers remained seated, smoke
curling from fresh cigarettes, as they rehearsed
their whiplash stories.

A dog yipped nearby, prompting others to yip and
bark in response. Nothing here to justify abandoning
my La-Z-Boy.

I returned to my **Herald** and read the list of hospital
admissions and drunk driving arrests
                    till drowsiness took over again.

In The College Cafeteria

this evening, my baked potato spoke to my stir-fry.
I swear it. This is no exercise for the Abnormal Psych
class. For it is a fact, a fact of reality, not a fact of my

psyche, that the steaming spud I slit open and dolloped
butter into, cried out, "Stir fry! Help!" Personally, if I
were a potato, I would have cried out to another starchy

foodstuff, or maybe for something lean and orange like
a carrot or yam. I would've yelled, "Carrot!" and, if that
didn't work, I'd starch out, "Yam! Yam! Yam!" (Repeti-

tion reinforces the concept of distress, y'know.) And if I
were in really dire straits, I'd scream, "Carrot and yam,
come hither! Help!" Since that's a bit archaic-sounding,

I'd probably best shout, "Carrot and yam, I care, I yam!"
Or better yet, to guarantee the best help for a spud in a
pickle, I'd cry, "Fellow root crops, rise and cut off your

roots. Help!" or "Root crops unite and throw off your
roots!" Some call this teacher burnout. I call it a bagel.

G. Louis Heath, Ph. D.

ABOUT THE AUTHOR

G. Louis Heath, Ph.D., was born September 4, 1944 in mountainous Portola, California and raised in foothills Oroville, California. He earned his B.A., M.A., and Ph.D. degrees from the University of California at Berkeley. Retired from Illinois State University, he is now the chair of the Social Science Division, Mount St. Clare College, Clinton, Iowa, where he has been recently instrumental in establishing a Social Justice major. Among the courses he teaches at MSC are a seminar on Native Americans and an interdisciplinary class titled "Scandinavian Thought and Culture."

Dr. Heath has published eleven books, including most recently, **Leaves Of Maple: An Illinois State University Professor's Memoirs of 7 Summers Teaching In Canadian Universities, 1972-1978** and **Redbird Prof: Diary And Poems Of An Illinois State University Professor, 1969-1981.** Both were published by 1stBooks.com.

Professor Heath has long published short stories and poems in a wide variety of literary magazines. He is currently working on a novel.

Printed in the United States
791300001B

9 780759 614178